Death as a Side Effect

LATIN AMERICAN WOMEN WRITERS

Death as a Side Effect

Ana María Shua

Translated by Andrea G. Labinger

UNIVERSITY OF NEBRASKA PRESS | LINCOLN AND LONDON

La muerte como efecto secundario © Ana María
Shua, 1997. By arrangement with Literarische
Agentur Mertin Inh. Nicole Witt e. K.,
Frankfurt am Main, Germany.

Portions of the translation of chapters 1, 2, and 3
originally appeared in *The Dirty Goat* 19 (Fall
2008). An excerpt of the translation of chapter
26 originally appeared in *Two Lines: A Journal
of Translation* 13 (Spring 2006).

Work published within the framework of "Sur"
Translation Support Program of the Ministry
of Foreign Affairs, International Trade and
Worship of the Argentine Republic.

Publication of this book
was assisted by a grant
from the National
Endowment for the Arts.

NATIONAL
ENDOWMENT
FOR THE ARTS
A great nation
deserves great art.

Library of Congress
Cataloging-in-Publication Data
Shua, Ana María, 1951–
[Muerte como efecto secundario. English]
Death as a side effect / Ana María Shua;
translated by Andrea G. Labinger.
p. cm. — (Latin American women writers)
ISBN 978-0-8032-2807-8 (cloth: alk. paper)—
ISBN 978-0-8032-2989-1 (pbk.: alk. paper)
1. Argentina—Fiction. I. Labinger, Andrea G.
II. Title.
PQ7798.29.H8M9413 2010
863'.64—dc22   2010011416

Set in New Caledonia by Bob Reitz.
Designed by Nathan Putens.

ADVERSE REACTIONS: Rifampicin is well tolerated at recommended doses. The following adverse reactions have been reported: itching, skin redness, rash, loss of appetite, nausea, vomiting, abdominal pain, pseudomembranous colitis, diarrhea, hepatitis, and thrombocytopenia. The latter symptom may be accompanied by purpura and is associated with intermittent treatment; it is reversible if the drug is discontinued immediately.

Instances of cerebral hemorrhage and death have been reported when administration of Rifampicin was continued or reintroduced after purpura was noted.

Death as a Side Effect

1

If you look at a red square for a while and then stare at a piece of white paper, you'll see a green square. In exactly that way, like an optical illusion, like a sunspot dancing around my retina, flashing from negative to positive, bright and annoying before my eyes, I constantly saw the full-color photo of the tumor blocking my father's intestine.

I was tired. I hadn't slept much. Sleep has never been easy for me; I've always had to fool it, seduce it so it would overcome me. But in the last few years, sleep has become an unexpected luxury that I try to enjoy whenever it comes, without worrying about time or place, like a married lover.

I felt awful. My father's visit, his brief, brutal presence, had left me exhausted.

If you had been here with me, I would have shown you the photo. You would have looked away in disgust, with disapproval. But you're not here, and I need to share it with someone, even if it's only with my miserable memory of you.

It was an obscene photo, clearly pornographic in intent: not a single trace, not a single attempt at aesthetic expression, utter artlessness. It had been taken with a small camera at the end of a long, flexible tube, during a colonoscopy. It showed a wet, pink membrane that looked like the deformed, unthinkable inside of a woman's sex. The tumor was black, with rough edges. There was no transition, no progressive darkness leading to that abrupt change of color. Quite the opposite: it had a violently red outline, like something a child might have drawn with a marker to clearly separate the figure from the background, to trace its margin — it forced one to remember that the powerful border did nothing to halt its advance — and it was the only element in the photograph that suggested pain.

I turned on the TV so I could immerse myself in a brilliant world that would turn the fixed image on my retina into a dance of light and shadows. That's the theory, anyway: one nail pulls out another, one image erases another, one woman cancels out another's memory.

Remote control in hand, I closed my eyes to select randomly, and I decided to stick with whichever channel it landed on. I didn't want to be carried away by the sort of crazy impatience that makes us change channels in search of something impossible and marvelous, something that doesn't exist, something as unlikely as the Fountain of Youth or El Dorado, in pursuit of supreme entertainment, Nirvana, self-dissolution, a fruitless search that forces us to turn off the machine, convinced that there's nothing, absolutely nothing, among the hundreds of possibilities offered to us, deserving of our attention, of our intentions.

If, instead of voluntarily surrendering to chance, I had opted to make a choice, I would have watched the talk show hosted by Sandy Bell, that clever transvestite who took his name from a cartoon and who sometimes manages to hold my interest. But chance brought me the president's weekly broadcast instead. It was a distraction and a relief.

The poor man, his cabinet, his party members, all worked hard to attract the fleeting attention of viewers and voters by combining intelligent journalism with lots of musical numbers and comedy routines. Of course, it was mostly political propaganda, but the production wasn't bad. As a sign-off, that image we've grown so accustomed to seeing in commercials would appear: the president trying to keep his balance, precarious at first, but growing ever stronger as he manages to overcome obstacles and difficult situations.

Although these circus charades may seem ridiculous to you and me, ordinary people love their representatives precisely for that reason, for their personal efforts to entertain them, to make them forget their poverty, unemployment, and boredom for a while. Our politicians take charge of the people's happiness quite directly, with their very bodies, and the people respond with votes and love. By now, everyone, even misfits and lunatics, knows that our leaders aren't the ones leading us.

The president seemed worn out beneath his thick makeup, with that odd expression of rejuvenated old folks we've become accustomed to after so many years of cosmetic surgery. The typical bags were beginning to show again beneath his reddened eyes; he had a nasty pimple on his chin that base and powder couldn't conceal. It was a shame he had entrusted his face to second-rate professionals. I imagined myself working on those features: I could have done it so much better. The makeup artist hadn't considered the changes in lighting for each shot.

I watched that absurd program in the vague hope that you, too, might be watching it somewhere in the world, out of curiosity or nostalgia, along with me. Now, after so long, now that it doesn't matter anymore, I can tell you how much you're always present in everything I do or decide not to do. You used to love watching TV. I suppose you still do; I suppose you still channel surf for hours on end, looking for the Magic Potion and enjoying the quest, even though you may deny it. If I were to do the same thing, if I were to flip channels at random, we might never meet. By staying right here like this, with any given program, I can almost be sure that sooner or later your eyes will pass over the same place as mine, almost as if we were together, almost as if our gazes could touch.

My father left the photograph for me on the metal table. Did he forget it? At one time, he would have made several copies to distribute among his acquaintances. These days it's dangerous to appear very sick. At any rate, he doesn't have many acquaintances anymore. When you go on living beyond certain limits, there usually aren't many friends left to celebrate your victory.

It surprised me to hear his voice from the other side of the door. He rarely goes out. My mother never does; she's hardly left their apartment in the last few years. They should have gone into a Home long ago, but a combination of good health, prudence, and money has allowed them to retain a degree of freedom. You know how it is: you've

3

seen old guys beyond the age of independence walking in a shopping center—and despite the hair dye and the operations, you can tell by the way they're bent over, by the way they move their knees—their bones are usually so much older than their skin—you can be sure you're dealing with someone powerful, or at least very rich.

In my desperation to share everything that's impossible to share with you, I often told you about my father. You listened without hearing me, although not impatiently, and I never could quite figure out if you were bored. I, for my part, seized on every fragment, every vague word of yours that might have given me more information about your life, your tastes, your history. Learning, for example, that you've hated the color green ever since you were very young was an overwhelming fact. Each time I chose a gift for you, our secret forced me to reflect on your personality: my clandestine gifts had to look as though you had chosen them yourself. It was simple to give you books, CDs, videos of film classics or of those awful old movies that, for some reason, we both recalled and I knew how to get my hands on. But sometimes I felt the need to give you something that would bring me closer to your body. And then I'd choose a scarf, a belt, a silk blouse in any other color, hoping you'd appreciate how hard I'd tried to avoid green.

I spoke to you many times about my father, but words impose limits. You would have had to participate—by mistake or by design—in the games my father proposes, and which only he can win, in order to understand certain aspects of reality that words can't reproduce. I told you too much: it was logical that his power over me should have piqued your curiosity. Resting your head on my shoulder, with a distracted half-smile, you listened to me much more attentively than I ever dared imagine.

I opened the door and he came in, always just a bit above me even though now I'm about a head taller than he is. He had hired a taxi driver to bring him, a discreet young man who works for him and for other old guys with money. With intelligent subterfuge, the two of them clumsily leaning on one another, the driver helped him up the three front steps and into the elevator.

4

When I saw him moving like a metal robot with rusty hinges, like the Tin Woodman of Oz, I thought of my own arthritis and wondered—although I already knew the answer—if I'd have the courage to shoot myself before I became totally incapacitated. Those fundamental decisions that you put off until tomorrow, until one day your crooked index finger is no longer strong enough to curl around the trigger. Well, there are always tall buildings: flying is one of my favorite fantasies.

He was leaning on a cane. One part of his body controlled the rest, forcing him to bend over and press the cane more firmly against the floor with both hands. The pain didn't come from his legs but rather from his belly. At times he doubled over.

"My dear son," my father said, lying as usual. "I know you have money problems."

That was true.

But by that time he had already given me the photo; that is to say, he had already clearly established which of us had more problems, because even in that respect, even in the accumulation of misery, just as with everything else, my father always had to win. I felt torn between the brutal reality of his pain and the way he was trying to blackmail me.

The tumor obstructed almost all the light from his intestine. Until now he had gotten by with enemas, but he couldn't last much longer.

Panting between sentence and sentence, interrupting himself to catch his breath, my father kept talking, worrying about me.

"You're my son, I'm your father. We need to let bygones be bygones. Here's the most important thing," he said. "I want to help you."

He pulled out a stack of bills—ten thousand dollars, counted and wrapped by the machine at the bank—announced the amount, and laid it on the table.

"This money is for you. I'm not saying it's a gift because you've got your pride and also because I don't want your sister to think I'm taking away any of her share."

I had been about to reject it, in spite of the sweat covering his face with each spasm, but now I stopped myself.

5

"It's not a gift," he repeated. "It's a loan in dollars at 20 percent annual interest. I'll collect the first payment in advance. Count it all, please, and give me two thousand right now."

I was so surprised that all I could do was obey. I counted out two thousand dollars, separated them from the stack of bills, and handed them to him.

"You'll have to repay me," my father continued, "two thousand dollars a year, which you'll give me every year on my birthday. In ten years, you'll have paid me back the capital, that is, the ten thousand. And if I die before that, my dear boy, the debt is canceled."

Since I didn't know whether to thank him or tell him to go to hell, I took the money and kept it.

When he left, I discovered that I felt more touched than angry. It was just another game; once again he was playing at winners and losers. My father had made a ten thousand dollar bet against death. And this time he hadn't had time to load the dice.

I counted the money again. Exactly eight thousand.

2

The telephone woke me like a scream. It was my father. It was night-time. I called a taxi. There are several dangerous blocks between his house and mine, but in an armored car, I felt safe. Taxis are little fortresses on wheels, one of the few trustworthy institutions we've got left.

Until a few years ago, you could still walk in the city. When we started seeing each other, I allowed myself to dream that one day we would walk along the street together, that one day you wouldn't mind being seen in public with me. I even imagined holding your hand on some solitary stroll, caressing your short, delicate fingers, the sensitive oval of your fingernails. You didn't like your hands; you thought they were too small: you used to spread out your fingers, displaying them for me, comparing them with the size of your palms, criticizing their shortness. You didn't like them, but to me, your childlike hands on my chest were so beautiful—deceitful, touching, and perfect: yours.

To walk together. We could still do it, if you wanted to. Not just at shopping centers or in guarded neighborhoods: there are many walking tracks in the city, secured places that pretend to be ordinary neighborhoods where, for a modest fee, it's possible to wear yourself out walking, passing infinite—or finite—landscapes, almost real. Almost. Just like those artificial substitutes that replace natural foods. Good enough for those who never knew any different, and for them, even better than the Real Thing.

I'm getting old.

My father's voice on the phone sounded terrified. No way to know if he was pretending. Whenever I see him, I can almost always tell;

years of living with him have taught me to detect the difference, but his voice confuses me — it's too much like mine. Mama was there, as always, and so was his secret physician, as old and nasty as my father, and for that very reason quite trustworthy as long as their interests coincided. Never trust a decent man, my father taught me: he'll always be ready to betray you just to keep his conscience clear.

When I'm not driving, the motion of cars puts me to sleep. Even during that short trip, I fell asleep. The screeching of brakes jolted me awake. There we were at Goransky's studio, and already, from a prudent distance, the security guards were pointing their weapons at us. Logy with sleep, I had asked the taxi driver to take me there as quickly as possible. It's the address I repeat most often — except for my own — whenever I climb into a taxi. My last workplace. From outside, you can't see the vines.

You'd never guess what my job is with Goransky. You might think he hired me as a makeup artist for his new film project, and you'd be right, but only partially. That's how our relationship began. I have a surprise for you: I'm Goransky's latest — but not his last — scriptwriter.

At first the opportunity struck me as very strange. Every morning, I'd look in the mirror and think that my life had begun again: I was going to work on a film script. I think naïve enthusiasm was what kept me going afterward. You know how much movies mean to me. How many times did we recite movie plots to each other, happily entertaining ourselves with stories that were so unlike our own poor, limited one?

How pretentious of me! To think you'd remember my words, my gestures, my enthusiasm, as vividly as I remember the exact shade of your eyes, like dark honey, nearly transparent in the sunlight, almost black when shadow and desire widened your pupils.

I know, you don't need to interrupt me: I was about to tell you what happened last night when my father phoned me, terrified or maybe just pretending to be terrified. But there are so many hours of my life that I could never tell you about, so I don't care if I sound disconnected or digressive now, tugging at the fragile thread of my story till its resistance — or yours — weakens. For many years I lived only to tell you what was happening in my life, and my every action or thought was transformed, at the very moment it was happening, into the words I would use to describe it to you, as though including you in my story like that, even just as a listener, could somehow make all the randomness and confusion coherent and give meaning to the chaos of reality. Later on, for years after you'd gone, I gave in to that chaos, to the muck of history. I let the amorphous material we call life—or the memory of life—accumulate, knowing it can only be shaped in the telling, by choosing, sorting, or by introducing a cleverly encoded disorder whose key is given to the listener, the reader. I know you're probably eager to find out more, right now, about my father's urgent phone call, but I'm not going to tell you anything just yet. This is a deliberate digression.

Why did Goransky choose me as his scriptwriter? At first I didn't get it. He's a big shot—worshiped as an international movie personage around here, even though he's never filmed anything except that famous short subject in Antarctica.

These days, the only thing they're filming in this country is commercials. Just as at some point they stopped making umbrellas, they stopped making films. Of course, we still have our directors, our artists, our projects, our usual talent. The fact that they can never function in any concrete way is strictly a matter of circumstance, as everyone who has anything to do with the movie industry says. Those who have nothing to do with the movie industry don't give a damn about the whole business.

Goransky could afford his dreams. His outrageous personal fortune began to accumulate a few generations before he came along. But despite his great passion for film, my director would feel like less of a man if he used his own money to produce his picture. His personal prestige rides on finding investors willing to take a chance on his talent.

You'll understand why I was so excited when Goransky called: having a job is a privilege in the first place, and on a film script with the great director, no less. I envisioned myself in five-star international hotels, hidden in a corner of a reception hall in Berlin, in

Biarritz, ecstatically listening to the public's laughter and applause. It didn't matter that Goransky had never managed to finish a film: we would do it together. It didn't matter that my whole experience as a professional writer was limited to editing medical pamphlets: Goransky had noticed my hidden talent, and I wasn't about to disappoint him.

When he asked to see me, I thought he probably wanted to find out more about me as a makeup artist. At that point Goransky thought he had a nearly finished script, and he was chatting with each of the professionals he planned to hire. Later, I found out that this definitive step had been repeated several times.

I needed the work and presented my qualifications without waiting for questions. I began with a self-promotional explanation that I won't repeat for you—I use it so often: the sweep of a glance on the subject's face, the perception of its shape, its bone structure, and how it's possible, without changing them, to create a different optical illusion by working on the outer surface. I talked about my experience with photographers, with models, in various commercials. I talked too much, too naïvely. I didn't tell him until much later, for instance, something that really might have interested him: how I had arrived at my strange profession after experimenting with so many others, and how, ever since the bad times began, I had accepted any kind of job at all; how I devoted myself to making up old folks for family parties, making up dolls for rich little girls and lonely men, and once in a while even making up corpses for funeral homes.

Goransky didn't care too much about my previous experience as a makeup artist. He had read that story I published a few years ago in the Eudeba anthology, the first and only story I ever wrote in my life, which takes place on a military base in Antarctica. That unusual detail, the fact that it occurs in the frozen south, caused the story to be published and republished in many anthologies, even in other countries. These were collections in many languages with titles like: *In Icy Realms*, *Southernmost Stories*, *Tales of Exotic Places*, *Patagonia and Beyond*, or possibly *Tales from the End of the World*. Each time we heard about a new publication, my wife would nag me about my vocation as a writer, ruining my good mood with her annoying, demanding confidence in my nonexistent literary talent.

Goransky was fascinated by Antarctica. Someone showed him my story; he read it and wanted to meet me. And if he had originally thought of hiring me as a makeup artist, something in the way I expressed myself made him turn toward a different proposal: working together on a new film script.

"The book I have doesn't work for me. I want my next film to take place in Antarctica," he said. "And all the others as well. Antarctica, and lots of voice-overs: those are my trademarks, the Goransky seal," he explained, as though he already possessed a vast accumulation of movies to his credit.

The strange thing is that he could have been a film genius, at another time, in another place. From the very first day, his creative capacity drove me wild with enthusiasm. I would toss out the end of a ball of yarn, any old crap, and he would start pulling, turning it into the center of a film plot. His brain was a crazy gold mine of images. An enormous, heavy man with the brightest eyes you could ever imagine, in constant motion, a hippo on amphetamines, a bear hypnotized into thinking he was a squirrel. As we worked and I wrote, Goransky paced up and down the studio, breaking toothpicks with his huge hands, bending paper clips, moving chairs and decorations around, and climbing up and down the staircase that led to the terrace.

The studio was an enormous place, protected like a fortress, with reinforced doors and thick bars safeguarding all possible points of entry, in addition to the security guards who had been hired to watch over it night and day. At one side, as though they had been piled up carelessly, but really very deliberately displayed, were all the prizes he had won for his famous Antarctic short subject. Maybe we weren't so different after all.

In the great hall where we were going to work, vines grew wildly around the beams. It was winter: naked branches fell, and yet they seemed to contain such an aggressive vital force that I amazed myself by wanting to finish the film before spring.

Goransky took me to see the vehicles he kept in the underground garage. He had already bought much of the necessary equipment for filming: some enormous tractor sleds, specially designed for snow, imported from Oslo. And the astonishing Lapp huts on wheels, made in Japan.

All he needed was a good script. And I was the one chosen to write it. At that moment, I didn't think about my predecessors, among them professionals with better qualifications and more experience than I, writers, TV scriptwriters, publicists, journalists who had attempted the same thing I was about to attempt now. Goransky tossed all my doubts out the window.

"I'm tired of people who use the same old industry rhetoric," he told me. "They think they're creating a story and all they do is string clichés together like ducks roasting on a spit."

A strange remark—nobody around here eats roast duck, but for that very reason, it impressed me as a sign of his creative capacity. I liked the comparison: several ducks, all the same size, all dead and skinned, threaded on a long metal skewer, turning over a fire. The living image of a TV script.

"You work spontaneously; you think out of the box; you have broad vision: that's what I'm looking for."

But what *was* Goransky looking for? After so many months of working with him, I'm not so sure anymore. Spring came, and the vines proved to be nearly as dangerous as they appeared.

When we started, the protagonists were a couple of young kids, practically adolescents, who had gone to Antarctica as part of a research team. By the following week, they had been transformed into a father and his daughter, and shortly after that, into a pregnant woman. Each time we were about to complete the framework—or, rather, the theme—of a coherent story, Goransky would pull a brick out from under, and the structure fell down. He called me at 3:00 a.m.

"Everything we've got so far is good; we're doing fine," he said, trying to seduce me. "We'll hold on to that story, but instead of a pregnant woman, the hero needs to be a Saint Bernard."

You know where I live and how I live. Goransky pays me by the month, and to me, that money means the difference between survival and real life. He's one of the privileged few; only instead of making the world tremble with those colossal, violent parties that entertain the very wealthy, he invests his money in his movie, or, rather, in his dream of a movie. But he's already ordered the blank film, and every day he goes down to the basement to operate his vehicles, try them out again, oil them, test their movements.

At this point, our relationship is extremely tenuous; it's worn thin at several points, and the slightest abrupt move could break it. I no longer dream about international festivals; instead, I have obsessive, recurrent dreams about earning one more month's salary.

Those are my good dreams, my daytime reveries. My bad dreams haven't changed since then, since I dreamed them at your side: the sea, as usual. That immense wave forming on the horizon, seemingly motionless at first, because of its great distance: a foam-covered mountain. But it moves. Swiftly. Like a wave.

My father's desperate midnight phone call had led me through the tortuous paths of my mind to Goransky's studio. The taxi's screeching brakes saved me from drowning once more in the tidal wave of my dream. I was trying to free myself from what was left of the sea and reorient myself in the nightmare of reality when the studio security guards surrounded the car, aiming their weapons at us from a careful distance.

Since I had never been there at night before, I didn't know the evening security staff. Fortunately, one of them seemed to know me. He was a dark-skinned man with sad eyes and a face that a police artist might have created with an Identi-Kit: the sort of person you might have seen many times but would still be unable to describe. I showed my documents and demanded that they call Goransky, and in spite of the hour, they let me talk to him: they were trained to avoid complications. A couple of orders from him, and they were off my back.

It was still hot. The air from the street smelled of dampness, of earth and wet cement, of rotten fruit. One hour later, with my clothes soaked in sweat despite the taxi's air conditioning, I arrived at my father's house.

3

No one can humiliate you like your parents. No one else in the world has that tremendous power: the same power we have over our children. You don't have children—you didn't have any when you left, and I'm not interested in imagining your life beyond that moment—but you had parents: you understand what I mean.

No one can display your secret childhood fears in public like your parents. No one but they can remind you later, in your adulthood, of the promises you made in your youth, the ideals you embraced in adolescence.

No one knows your weaknesses as well as your parents do.

My legs are my weakness. Very skinny. "Emaciated legs," the pediatrician explained: a genetic trait that, according to him, could be modified with a bicycle. "For developing your muscles," he insisted. That's why, when I close my eyes, the first image that rises from the depths of my childhood isn't the flavor of a croissant dipped in milky coffee or the algae fragrance of summer: it's pedaling. A pedaling sensation that tickles the soles of my feet and creeps up my entire body and makes me lean over the handlebars a little, just enough to cut the wind that's begun to tousle my hair, gently, free of the oppressive superiority of adult hands.

Not only was I young once, but I also had hair, although you never saw it. With hair on my head and a bicycle between my legs, I was a centaur on wheels, wheels that were both my joy and my misfortune, because while my leg muscles grew quite strong, my calves and thighs stayed as oddly skinny as they were at the beginning, as always, as they are now. Like the scrawny little ankles peeking out of the flared trouser legs of Alfred Jarry's Superman. When I was an adolescent, I discovered and fell in love with surrealism because of those ankles that looked so much like mine. I'm still embarrassed to take off my pants for the first time in front of a woman.

Of course, that was one of my father's favorite ways of humiliating me—so simple, so convenient, so easy to justify to others.

"What are you doing in those long pants, son? Go take them off—we're at the beach."

Or at the swimming pool, or the club, or the river, or any other place where, in a sufficiently loud voice, it might be possible to attract the stares of everyone around, especially women. Adults who, as a single voice, would bemoan their neighbor's problem—such a nice man, so good-looking—and that skinny, stubborn, boring son, that kid who didn't seem interested in anything but his bike and who refused, or at least was reluctant to, perform one of the most logical acts on earth: taking off his pants at the beach. Showing his legs.

I arrived at my father's house an hour after his urgent call, feeling like I deserved it all, even my past. He opened the door himself. He was feeling better. I walked in, thinking he was going to insist that I show my legs, as skinny and pathetic as always. However, he simply stared at me silently for a few moments. Then he pointed toward my mother and the doctor with a glance.

"And *this*," he said, as if the others didn't know me, "is my son."

And that's how it was, exactly the same: as if he were saying, Take off your pants, you wretch.

My sister Cora wasn't there. My father's victim and parasite, she enjoys both the privileges of a child and the rights of an adult: she lives in my parents' house, but she's never there when she's needed. I spoke with the secret physician. He had reached the limit of what he could do without an infrastructure. The tumor blocked almost all the light from my father's rectum. God knows why doctors refer to light when they talk about any hole, no matter how dark and smelly. Now he was recommending admitting him as an inpatient.

It wasn't an easy decision. If they operated on him, he had almost no chance of surviving. It was unlikely that a man his age could withstand such a fierce operation: they would have to cut out a piece of his intestine and construct an artificial anus. A hole in his belly through which shit could gently flow, pushed along by peristaltic motion. If the piece they cut out wasn't too big, if everything turned out better than expected, there'd be another operation, which is usually performed shortly after the first one these days; they would join the two loose ends of gut, and my father would get his sphincter back. But the recovery period would be very long; he would be laid up for a long time, and once he entered the hospital, no one could prevent them from sending him to a Home.

People live a long time in Convalescent Homes, but nobody ever recovers enough to get out of one.

My father's other option was to explode in his own shit and die. To forget the operation and let the obstruction grow, swelling his intestines with bits of poorly digested food, more and more poorly digested, mixed with epithelial cells, until the accumulation of fermented material reached his stomach, producing vomit laced with shit, and the gas pressure finally caused some weak point in his (at that point) scar-covered intestinal wall to mercifully explode, spilling the material into his abdominal cavity in a final, benevolent peritonitis.

It was a question of choosing between the operation—and consequently the Home—or exploding, or suicide.

The secret physician pretended to comfort my mother. It's not unusual for these types to be in collusion with the Convalescent Homes. The money they collect isn't just for their medical services, but more importantly for their silence, the good grace not to report any illness or incapacity.

Mama's gaze was opaque, indifferent. She's always lived a little like that, wrapped in a sort of cloud that masks her senses and feelings—especially pleasure and happiness—but one that also obscures colors and certain aspects of reality. Nonetheless, I was surprised not to see her wringing her hands in desperation, not surrendering to pain, the only sensation that kept her lucid. At that moment I didn't yet realize what was happening. Cora should have warned me.

Convalescent Homes. A logical name. Politically correct terminology is spreading throughout the world, banishing cruel truths from the language and replacing them with euphemisms that are more tolerable to humanitarian sensibilities. Why say what can be insinuated? I can still recall a time when they were called old age homes, and later geriatric centers and senior residences or simply residences, and of course they weren't exactly the same thing as the Convalescent Homes: they weren't mandatory.

Convalescent Homes are a world within a world, an area of life that nobody who hasn't entered one can ever know completely, just as you and I together discovered the ephemeral world of secret love.

A spasm of pain distorted my father's face. His intestinal contractions affected his vagus nerve, causing him cold sweats, nausea, and faintness, in addition to pain. He'd choose suicide, of course. We had discussed it many times. Now bargaining with the secret physician would begin: how much for a quick, happy death, how much for a slightly longer, or more painful, one, and whether it wouldn't be better for him, in the long run, to jump off the balcony and die free of charge, in order to leave your mother better provided for, my father would tell me. I didn't want to hear it; I wasn't ready to deal with it.

It was 4:00 a.m. In the heavy air, other people's sweat seemed to condense and filter into my lungs, and from time to time, the sound of a car in the street below tore through the silence. It had been difficult for my parents to remain independent and free on such a high floor, with such frequent blackouts. But cats and old folks don't like to abandon their turf.

"You're not going to have an operation," I said, trying to start a conversation that pity had postponed longer than necessary. I said it just like that, with no question mark at the end; it seemed so obvious to me.

"You're in a big hurry for your father to die. Go sit down; it'll be a while yet," Mama interrupted for the first time.

I ignored her this time, just as he had always ignored her. Papa didn't answer me right away. He looked at the glass cabinet filled with an assorted array of small objects that they had collected on their trips, resting both hands on the table, which was covered with glass and a cloth that protected the glass, and finally a sheet of plastic, to keep the cloth from getting dirty. He rested both hands there and stood up. Suddenly lightened, thrown off-balance, the chair fell backward. The doctor hurried to turn it upright. For years now, those chairs, with their too-heavy backrests, had lost their original stability. Slowly, without looking at me, Papa went to the kitchen and returned with a glass of milk and some cold, leftover tripe stew he found in the refrigerator. He sat down to eat it with a spoon.

"Are you hungry?" I asked, astonished.

"Eating is good. I ate an early dinner, and now it's dawn. Eating is life," my father said. "Just look at yourself, so scrawny. You don't have enough weight on you to fight against the world."

"How marvelous your dad is, with that amazing vitality of his," the doctor commented, as if he believed it was still possible to get a little something extra, a tip, in that house.

"If only you'd have gotten a teaching degree," Mama said, suddenly. "At least you'd have a career. Then we could leave this world peacefully."

It was a very strange remark to make to a man who had crossed life's midpoint, someone who had gotten through the most important part of his life without the need to get a teaching degree. I didn't know how to reply, so I kept talking to Papa.

"Are you going to let them operate on you? And then go to a Home?"

"People with debts," my father said, "are the ones who usually want to die. For those of us who are creditors, life is worthwhile. I've still got a lot to collect."

4

Must I keep pretending I'm writing to you? Must I continue to dupe myself into believing that someday you'll read all this, just as I used to pretend to be interested in other women in order to keep pace with what you felt, or what you said you felt, for your husband? Sometimes I got tired of it; sometimes I preferred to invent stories, to lie to you rather than keep deceiving myself. Sometimes I didn't feel like faking even simple pleasure or amusement—much less happiness—with those women, so I got rid of them with polite words and brusque gestures, knowing I'd never call them again, looking for excuses to avoid causing them any more pain than necessary. Sometimes now I even get fed up with you, the fact that you're always there, an indifferent, indispensable witness to my life. Seeing me although you're not looking at me, reading me although you can't read me, conjured by my writing, ignoring me with the disarming coldness of mirrors that reflect us with feigned fascination while returning only our own gaze.

While Goransky and I understand that our society doesn't work, that we'll never give birth to that impossible, desired story or even manage to conceive it, I continue meeting with him three times a week. Our relationship is nurtured by a routine I don't dare interrupt: a single absence would be enough to end it.

In this crazy November heat the air conditioning in Goransky's studio demands justice: according to the calendar, it's still spring. Why does the weather in this city always take us by surprise? Why is it so hard for us to remember its vagaries, as if up till now, it's been a model of predictability? Was it so hot this time last year, we ask ourselves as though we'd never been here before, as though we'd just arrived, convinced that our environment is becoming unfairly tropicalized.

I'm talking about the weather because I don't want to talk about my father.

The operation to remove the tumor and a good portion of my father's intestine was set for that afternoon, and there I was, trying to forget about my confused feelings among the overgrown vines in Goransky's studio, dreaming à duo about delirious Antarctic adventures that would never materialize.

I was hungry when I arrived. I'm trying to save money, even on food, since now, for security reasons, I can't dip into my taxi fund, but I'm not resigned to the idea of cheap substitutes, the consistency of propylene glycol, hydrogenated soybean oil that permeates the flavor of canned foods. Goransky was waiting for me with sandwiches on white bread: like any good seducer, he had familiarized himself with my needs and tastes. It was hard for me to concentrate, though. I was very upset, not only about the operation that afternoon but also because I had been attacked again on the way over.

I was ambushed at a traffic light. No one stops for red lights at night anymore, but I didn't realize they were attacking in the daytime as well. The first time I saw a driver deliberately ignore a red light was one night in Porto Alegre. I didn't think our city would reach that point so quickly. (We don't believe that our city, so prosperous, so proud, could ever reach that point.) The cab driver seemed accustomed to it: he told me that daytime attacks are a frequent new development. He kept going resolutely, running over one of the kids in the process.

"Don't worry," he told me. "These guys used up all their bullets just fooling around. When they have ammo, they don't wait for you to stop—they shoot at the tires."

He must have been right, because they didn't do anything. Through the rear window, I saw a few of them pick up the wounded man and carry him off as best they could.

I'm no good at this. At being a screenwriter, I mean. I'm not a good architect of words; I don't know how to design a structure that can organize the story. There must be some reason I chose or was chosen for this peculiar career as a makeup artist, a job I really love, although I must admit, sometimes with embarrassment, that it's a job for homosexuals or women.

I am, I think of myself as, a makeup artist. I need to work on flesh, on skin. And what Goransky was asking me to do was to construct a skeleton using only one rib: a synopsis, that initial outline of what the film might turn out to be. But instead of concentrating on the structure, I have a tendency to go straight for the makeup, the style, the adjectives: as if, having found a skull, I was supposed to focus on painting the outline of the eyes instead of trying to build a spine to hold the head up. This is a job for specialists, and if at first Goransky had tried to convince me that my freshness and spontaneity were what he was looking for, by now he realized he'd been mistaken.

It's no accident either that he hasn't gotten any farther along with his story by working with more experienced people. It's not that we're having problems with dialogue, character definition, or plot. The problem is simpler and more serious than that: we still haven't managed to determine what the theme of the film is going to be.

I'm older than Goransky, but his power, his control of money, makes me feel like a kid when I'm with him. To have plenty of money and to be accustomed to managing it: this is a level of adulthood not all of us achieve. He's a good person, though, and when I manage to keep my mind off his delirium, I appreciate and confide in him. I told him about my father, and for a moment he seemed to listen to me like a friend. But immediately, he got all excited about the idea of filming an operation in Antarctica, one of those typical medical emergency things that usually grab the viewer's attention.

I tried to follow along as he tentatively dreamed up illnesses and operations, one by one, for all the characters, the unlikely characters in the film, and I tried to calculate the effects that operation might have on our vague story. Did I say I felt like a kid when I was with him? Maybe that's not the exact feeling. I feel small under his sway, but not like a boy under his father's control, more like a toy in a baby's hands. Toward noon, I had had enough and wanted to collect my pay. Sometimes I think he pays me just to listen to him. Since he can't actually make his film, at least he has someone to tell it to in all its infinite, potential variety. Like someone who invites you to walk though the garden of forking paths, but without choosing: following all of them methodically, infinitely.

Does this interest you? Shall I go on? Your silence ought to be enough, the fact that you're not interrupting me. But it's never enough; anyone who's gone through this overwhelming kind of love understands. Do you adore me? I would ask you when we were together. You laughed at me. Soap opera dialogue. You're not supposed to say you adore me; you're supposed to say you love me. But for me, it wasn't the same thing. You can love your kids; you can love (sometimes) your parents. I think I even loved my wife sometimes. You can love a dog, a friend. I needed to know—and no answer was good enough—if you adored me. Just like that, like in a soap opera. Right now I don't feel like mentioning or describing your body, but that's what I meant, what I would have wanted to ask you. Whether your body felt the same turmoil, the same uneasiness, the same disconnection, when it was apart from mine.

I'm going around in circles, following all the possible curves, and all I do is trace a single, flat spiral that always brings you back—brings *us* back?—to the only possible center: my father.

Morphing from secret physician into official physician without any need to change his disguise, the doctor signed the order to admit my father to the hospital where they would operate on him. I went there directly from Goransky's studio. If everything turned out well—what a strange word!—in a few days, they would take him from the hospital to the Convalescent Home.

My father thought buying health insurance was a ridiculous expense. He preferred to depend on what was left of the state system of benefits for retirees. The hospital building was in bad shape; there were very few nurses, but the medical care was good. Margot was waiting for me at the entrance.

Your name comes right out of a tango, I told her when we met. But Margot's real name wasn't Margarita, like in the tango, but rather Márgara, which is even worse. I'll tell you about her some other time: you always loved the trendy perversion of hearing about my other relationships. Margot seemed happy. It's so important to women that we let them participate physically in our misfortunes, as if revealing a weakness were the most convincing proof of our love. Being allowed to accompany us to a loved one's wake, to cheer us up in a surgical waiting room, means much more to you women than an invitation to a party.

I arrived in time to kiss Papa goodbye—perhaps for the last time—before they wheeled him into the operating room. As old as he is, I still envy that large, heavy body of his, with its glowing skin that the nurses find so hard to handle. But lying there naked, without his glasses, false teeth, or hearing aid, he looked helpless. A mind separated from the world, a body subjected to hard-to-identify sensations. As I approached, he grabbed me with one arm, forcing me to lower my head toward his mouth.

"The lawyer has the papers, Ernie, but there's also the little ledger book under one of the bathroom tiles."

He had an old man's dank bad breath, and he was talking to me about money. I stood up, relieved. Mama regarded us with a baffled expression I didn't understand. Then my sister arrived, running, panting, late as usual. She hugged me. Poor Cora: she never escaped from the cage. She couldn't even pretend to have an independent existence, as I did.

Mama looked at the three of us: Margot, me, and Cora with her windblown hair and frightened expression.

"You, the three of you, are you related?"

"Mama," I replied, calmly, but with anguish and astonishment, "this is Cora. I'm Ernesto—we're sister and brother. Don't you remember? We're your children."

"And her?" pointing to Margot.

"She's my girlfriend."

Mama looked at us with great tenderness. She caressed Cora's cheek, as Cora tried not to cry. Margot, on the other hand, must have felt happy, but didn't show it out of a sense of obligation. What an amazing opportunity: to be a part of such an intimate scene.

"How nice!" Mama said. "What big children I have!" Suddenly, she seemed confused. "But then I must be very old."

She looked at me again, very carefully, as if trying to decide if it was possible to challenge such a grown-up son.

"Son, it's not right for you to have a girlfriend at your age. Shouldn't you have a wife and kids? Shouldn't you have given me grandchildren by now?"

It wasn't just her memory. She was crazy. Who knows for how long. I thought about those dark glances, eyes that emerged from the depths of a fog. It wasn't cataracts or old age. My mother had gone crazy quietly, like almost everything else she had ever done, and I hadn't even noticed.

5

My father smells of shit. Among the medicinal, antiseptic, soapy odors of the Intensive Care unit, it's possible to detect a faint trace that grows stronger as you approach his bed. On top of his perforated abdomen, a plastic bag collects his scant, yellowish semiliquid excrement with its jagged borders. A horrible, bloody gash connects his belly to his now-useless anus.

The operation was a success.

The surgeon was in a good mood, so he let us see him before he went to Intensive Care: Papa was awake, surprisingly lucid.

"You thought I croaked this time," he said with incredible glee. Pale, disheveled, with the face of a corpse and a voice like distant bells. "It'll be a while before you get rid of the old man!"

By the next day in Intensive Care, his happiness had diminished. There's no place lonelier than Intensive Care. They allowed my mother and me inside. She went over to him with an extraordinarily sweet expression on her face.

"My strawberry, my jewel, my diamond," she said to him, pushing tubes and wires out of the way so she could kiss his face. "Never forget, I love you so much."

Papa turned his face away.

"Get her off me."

I practically had to wrench my mother away from the bed. She started to cry.

"Where's the man I love? There's a disgusting, smelly old man in this bed. You can't fool me—I know my husband very well: he's a good-looking boy who likes to kid around."

"Mamita." I stroked her hair, so white it gleamed. "Look at him. You were just talking to him. He's my father."

Mama looked at me harshly, like I was someone making a stupid joke at a critically painful moment.

"Your papa? So what? If a disgusting old man is your papa, that doesn't mean he's my husband."

Once again, tears flooded her cataract-veiled eyes, forming little puddles in the dams of her wrinkles.

"Someone stole my man. I'll find him. Today I opened the bureau drawers and I felt better because he left all his clothes: that means he's coming back."

She was right. Why should she believe that broken-down old man was her husband? After all, was that poor old madwoman the lovely young mother I had been so proud of at school? What's crazy is the stupid logic that insists identity must remain the same through time and misfortune: as if, without you, I were still the same person.

When it came time for us to leave, I found out why my sister had refused to enter the room. As I stroked his forehead to say goodbye, Papa begged me not to go, to stay with him, not to leave him alone again. At the same time, without my realizing it, he hooked one of his arthritic fingers into the buttonhole of my jacket. When I tried to stand up, I found myself trapped. I thanked the cruelty of Intensive Care for forcing me to leave. A nurse helped me extricate myself.

My sister, on the other hand, had never managed to disentangle herself from the hook that had trapped her since birth. Cora came to fill the ever-growing space between my parents, destined to become ensnared with Papa in a skein of love and hatred that eventually absorbed all her vital energy. She never was able to leave home; she never managed to invent a history for herself other than the one that had been planned for her, that sterile life for which they, at the same time, reproached her, rubbing her failure in her face.

Papa had employed all his resources to exercise control and power over us: he tormented us with guilt, chastised us with punishment. When we were little, he applied the force of his physical strength, and when we were grown, he used the force of his money. He was able to combine the torturer's domain with that of the victim. He controlled us with lies, truth, intelligence, and a judicious knowledge of our weakness and desires. He also loved us: deeply. For himself alone.

One night, when my sister was fifteen, she arrived home after her curfew. She found Papa lying flat on the floor, his eyes rolled up into his head. He was dying, moaning with the death throes of a drowning victim. Cora let out a harrowing scream. Later we learned that Mama was locked in the bedroom. I woke up and dashed from my room, trying to help. Papa's heart appeared to be beating normally. Maybe just a touch of arrhythmia. I was in the process of calling an ambulance when his hand slammed down the receiver.

"Did you suffer?" he asked Cora, who was weeping in asthmatic anguish. "Is it sad to lose a father? Did it hurt you? That's how it hurt me when you didn't come home. Just like that—I thought you were dead, too!"

Sometimes I wonder if knowing you were dead would hurt me more than this, more than your deliberate absence, your abandonment. I think so. My capacity for jealously has misled me; I thought it would be more intense. I should be throwing up in pain to think that another man had so much more than your body—and your body, too—but all I can think of are the roads that took you away from me. While our relationship lasted, I was hardly ever jealous of your husband. You spoke of him often; you spoke well of him; you loved him. I loved him too, like an old friend: I knew, without knowing him, that in spite of everything, we were partners, we complemented one another. I knew our destinies were joined and that if one day you decided to leave, to live with someone else, that man wouldn't be me. Just as he and I needed one another, you would throw us both aside at the same time. I couldn't have anticipated that the third man would be so impossible, destructive, and close at hand that you wouldn't run away *with* him, but *from* him.

The days spent in Intensive Care give us time to get on with our own lives. It's the only place in the hospital where patients can depend on the kind of care that makes their relatives' presence unnecessary, at least from a strictly physical point of view. Contrary to what one might think, not too many employees are needed: just one nurse can control several stations simultaneously. As long as the readouts on the screens are normal, whatever happens to the patients is unimportant.

In a not-very-secret part of my heart, I wished Papa a sweet death, and I didn't feel guilty about that.

Cora doesn't want to put our mother in a Convalescent Home. In theory I agree, but in practice it's hard to conceal her condition. Yesterday Mama threw a pot of stew down the stairs. Any neighbor could report her. Legal protocol has created a kind of social benefit by relieving relatives of the burden of determining their old folks' fate. Those citizens who obey the law are uncomfortable with the ones who try to evade it.

Now that my father is in the hospital, Mama and Cora could eat something more interesting than those flophouse stews, but it's too late for them: they've stocked up on absurd quantities of beans, rice, polenta, and other cheap, nonperishable foods. Hundreds of empty boxes are piled up on the kitchen furniture. Cora showed me a box filled with pieces of paper—automatic teller receipts—organized in stacks held together with rubber bands. My father used to amuse himself by requesting receipts at the automatic teller so he could use the back of them for scrap paper.

In the Intensive Care unit, visiting hours are very strict. They only allow two half-hour visits per day. When the patient is awake, a half hour is nothing in the face of such loneliness, but when he's asleep, it can be too long for the relatives. A half hour of eternity in a corner of hell. Cora keeps refusing to enter the ward, making different excuses. Margot, on the other hand, tediously insists on accompanying me. Helping me in this helpless situation allows her to entertain all sorts of fantasies about our future: if I need her enough, I don't even have to love her. Poor Margot, a suffocatingly good woman. If her capacity for revenge is anything like her capacity for sacrifice, it must be hideous. I really should be wary of her generosity, but it's too comfortable for me to refuse.

This morning Margot and I went into the ward together. Papa was sleeping or unconscious. They didn't offer us too many explanations. In the bed to his right, there was a young man whose face had been deformed by blows and wounds. Suddenly, he began to breathe heavily, producing a loud, hoarse noise. As if emerging from the tiled floor, a man appeared with a video camera and started filming him. The nurse dropped the movie magazine she had been looking at and stood up, unhurriedly, to throw him out, almost giving him enough time to finish his job.

I took advantage of the incident to leave without attracting attention. Margot stayed a while longer. During this long half hour, the patients' relatives—there are very few of us; most of the patients are alone—stare at one another, monitoring each other to make sure no one escapes early without fulfilling his quota of revulsion and fear.

The man with the camera hadn't gone far. There he was, in the waiting room, ready to react to some signal that had doubtless been prearranged with the nurse. We chatted without any hope of killing time, barely distracting ourselves to make it pass. He complained about his job. Freelance cameramen don't get a salary, and there are thousands of them in the city, a plague, all of them competing among themselves and with amateurs, trying to capture those slice-of-life images than have almost entirely replaced fiction. There's one in every Intensive Care unit, and the arrangement they make with the nurses allows them not only to lie in wait but, more importantly, to prevent others from encroaching on their turf. This particular one was an authentic fan of Old Hollywood and considered his job a necessary evil.

"I don't understand why people don't want to see more movie deaths. Real death is boring, stupid," the man protested. "They go into a deep coma, and they stop breathing—that's all. It's rare to get a really good death scene on tape."

Margot sat out my quota in Intensive Care. I waited for her at the hospital entrance, in the sheltered area that protected people from the beggars. She came home with me. You'd have to see her: even though she's not young, she's more than pretty. She moves with natural grace, a demeanor that doesn't fade with the years. Margot reminds me of a deer: a gazelle that's lived beyond her reproductive days without having lost the touching dewiness in her eyes, the supple awkwardness of her impossibly long legs, and especially that nearly physical sensation of shyness: as if she were about to run away—or run off and hide inside herself—at any moment. I did what I was supposed to do, fastidiously, undressing her slowly, a distant spectator of her pleasure.

If I had been able to act that way with you, with that wisdom, that distance, could I have had you as I have Margot, much more in love than a man can accept without getting bored? Was it just my passion that made you different? And yet sometimes I think Margot hates me, that she's just waiting for the right opportunity to pay me back with the same indifferent courtliness.

"Your dad is dying. Tonight, if you ask me. He's very old, and his heart won't be able to take it," Margot said to me afterward, thinking she was giving me good news, while she pretended to smoke one of those little plastic tubes full of God-knows-what that gives off a gentle puff of steam with each breath.

She was waiting for me to sigh, for some sign that would express grief and relief at the same time, but I couldn't: suddenly, death appeared to me in all its misery; eternity breathed into my ear. I was lying on the big pillow, your favorite. I looked down and adjusted my farsighted eyes to focus on my graying chest hair, much grayer than the hair on my head or in my beard. I'm too close to old age to think about death—any death—with unmitigated relief.

I'm afraid.

6

If it weren't so painful, if it didn't hurt so much, watching my mother's madness would fascinate me, especially in the way it differs from fictional psychosis: those mad geniuses, coherent and creative, who face their doctors with a world view that's more just or more poetic than mediocre normality. Madmen who, in general, are used as a vehicle to express the author's or film director's world view. Happy lunatics for whom sanity would only mean monotony or misfortune.

Watching those movies or plays that show such intelligent, sane forms of dementia, you wonder why those brilliant crazies, so unfairly locked up, can't just pretend to be sane enough at the right moment to earn back their freedom. No one who's ever worked with a real psychotic would ask himself that ridiculous question. The foundations of memory break down and the files get all scrambled. Nothing can be found when it's needed; no programs exist to retrieve the appropriate answers at the critical time.

I'll never be able to read or see anything like that again without feeling outrage rise from my gut like a wave of nausea. In the circle of madness, all creative possibilities are abolished. My mother's delirium is repetitive, painful. Over and over she receives the news that Papa is gravely ill, that he had an operation, that he's in the hospital, that we don't know if he'll survive. "Cancer!" she repeats, bringing her hand to her brow and then to her chest. And she bursts out crying. Ten minutes later, she asks us again if we've heard from Papa, if he's left any message. She calls Cora and me aside, interrogating us separately.

"Do you think . . . a man his age . . . with a young girl?" she asks, looking me in the eyes to determine whether or not I think so. "But why am I asking you this when you're a man, just like him?"

She continues with Cora. "Your father didn't come home last night, and I wish it were an accident, but it's not. I wish it were!" and she emits the same agonizing sobs with which she responds to the words "illness," "tumor," "operation," "hospital."

If her madness brought her any peace at all, if it were easier, less terrible, for her to accept my father's voluntary abandonment than his illness, I would understand. Dementia as a means of masking a painful truth. I wish I could go crazy, people say when they're sane and suffering, but they don't know what they're talking about. Madness doesn't bring any relief: Mama is upset, she's suffering; she breathes painfully, expelling air from her chest with distressing effort. She opens and closes bureau drawers, sifting through them; she's can't resign herself to the repugnant idea she may have feared all her life, which craziness has now planted in her brain: the thought that her husband finally got tired of her once and for all.

My efforts to repeat her words make them sound false. It's impossible for a sane person to replicate a crazy one's delirium. Madness is like a nightmare, and dreams can't be described without transforming them, falsifying them. There's a breakdown in logical connections, holes in the discourse, in the signified as well as in the signifier. Sometimes the sick person can't find certain simple words in his head, so he counts on his listener to fill in the holes in that sieve through which meaning escapes. "You understand what I mean," Mama says, like a refrain. "You already know that," she tells us. "As you can imagine," she says, trying desperately to use her listener's mind to suspend bridges of meaning across crumbling cliffs, the disintegration of language.

Someone must have reported her, because a social worker showed up at Mama's apartment with two guards from a Convalescent Home. Cora had a long chat with her while Mama stared at them bug-eyed.

My sister made no attempt to fool the social worker; it would have been impossible. The secret physician had been prescribing sleeping pills for Mama, and hallucinations were a side effect. At times she watched her daughter talking to the social worker, who was seated at the table drinking hazelnut-flavored tea substitute, while the guards stood by the door. At other times, Mama changed her tactics, protecting herself with abrupt movements from something or someone unpleasant, which, although not frightening, seemed to be gaining on her. Those are probably the worst moments for those of us who live outside her world.

Keeping an older person at home in that condition is forbidden, severely punished, and unfavorably looked upon by most of society. But everything can be arranged. The social worker was one of those people whose principles won't allow them to accept money, so she left my parents' house with a lovely piece of French porcelain — as a child, I was intrigued by the way the artist imitated the filigree effect of the lace — probably the only knickknack of any real value that my parents owned.

It wasn't a solution — just a respite. There would be other accusations, other social workers. The guards had remained outside this time, but people said they were incorruptible: paid by the Home, not the State. I spoke with Cora. Why were we so determined to keep our parents out of a Convalescent Home? Nothing could be worse for Mama than that inner world into which she was sinking deeper and deeper. Our father wouldn't survive, I told Cora; he'd never leave Intensive Care alive: his old heart was too worn out. I used Margot's arguments to convince her, but it wasn't easy. Who's so naïve as to imagine that every slave wants to be free of his master?

We continued arguing in the taxi on the way to the hospital via the safest route. When we arrived, we found out that Papa was out of Intensive Care and that they had moved him to a room. He was better. Recovering.

The old man's tough, I thought to myself, flooded with joy. I knew they couldn't get rid of the old son of a bitch that easily! I looked at Cora, who was smiling as stupidly as I was. Not only was I happy, I felt a tremendous desire to phone Margot and show her how wrong her well-meaning prediction had been. See, you idiot, see? I was right. See? The problem wasn't so easy to get rid of.

Now the most complicated part begins. There are two other patients in Papa's room who depend on the outside to survive. The hospital doesn't provide food. Outside the Intensive Care wards, each nurse must attend to dozens of patients. Only the poor go to hospitals, which are turning out to be a horrible private enterprise. The franchise owners have to restrict their services—personnel, food, bedding, medication—so that their outlay for equipment will be profitable. Surrounded by peeling, shabby hallways, flooded bathrooms, and piles of trash, the beautiful glass and steel equipment gleams like sculpture, waiting to be admired by the humble patients. Nobody—and especially no one with an elementary school education and minimal resources—would ever agree to check into a hospital that didn't boast equipment of adequate quantity and quality, machines with impressive names, with screens and windows and colored beams and chrome tubing and tiny television cameras.

My father wasn't in his new room. At each side of his used but empty bed, like the good and bad thieves, was a patient, one recalcitrant and the other repentant. On the left side, out cold, an old man slept with his mouth agape, false teeth dangling and a thread of foamy saliva trickling from the corner of his lips. On the right, a young man protested and defended himself as his brother or friend forced him to swallow some light broth. The patient rejected the food, and the boy who was serving him swallowed spoonful after spoonful, trying to tempt him or set an example, as mothers do when their children refuse to eat: Mmm, look, it's delicious, see how I'm eating it? In fact, he was finishing up the meal with obvious gestures of pleasure.

"Are you the son? They took him away for a little while," the boy told me. "He's having an IVS."

"IVS?"

"In-tra-video-scope," he mumbled with difficulty, his mouth full of soup.

We hurried over to the IVS room. They had placed Papa inside a shiny, new device. Standing in front of the screen that showed the workings of my father's internal organs, a doctor was lecturing to no one in particular, as if he were talking to himself. In reality, he was directing his remarks to other patients, some accompanied by relatives, who were awaiting their turn on stretchers or in wheelchairs.

I listened for a while. There were many words I didn't understand, not all of which were medical jargon. Soon my thoughts carried me far from the doctor's speech, and yet I kept staring at the screen. Then, without intending to, precisely because of that mental wandering effect, I realized that the chaotic, brilliant image pulsing rhythmically on the screen was a recording that repeated again and again and which surely would start over every time the device was turned back on. Surely that's what the IVS is for: to convince the patients of the high technological quality of the services provided by that shabby institution. Even the most impoverished hospitals compete fiercely for secret physicians and healers, since they have to meet a certain patient quota in order to receive their state subsidy.

Now I want to tell you how I felt when I realized my father was going to survive, that he would have another operation and be transferred to a Home. It's not pleasant, but I'm going to write it anyway. I want you to know as much about me as I know about myself: to surrender myself in writing with the same illusion of abandon that you achieved when you gave your body to me, and which dissipated so quickly afterward: because I never really could tell where you were, where you were escaping to at the very moment your final cry was extinguished, your final shudder completed. You would disappear without leaving my side, your childlike hand on my chest, and maybe that was what fascinated me most: that I could be inside you so many times and never really have you.

I want to tell you something even worse, the most offensive thing I see in myself, without even concealing the generosity in that fake, cruel expression I use when I try to fool you, or myself, into believing I'm being objective. I want to tell you about my sick pleasure, mixed with childish delight, at the fact that my father is still alive. The idea that now he's going to suffer, the idea that, completely restrained and unable to defend himself, this time he's going to pay for everything.

My torturer, tied to the rack.

7

When I heard the banging and the explosions, I did what we all do: I made sure the security features in my apartment were working. I played music full blast so I wouldn't hear the screams; I locked myself in the bathroom and turned on the shower. Sitting on the toilet, miserable, I analyzed the mathematical probability that the vandals—professional thieves don't make noise—would get into my apartment.

I would have loved to take a shower to get rid of the smell of fear, but I'd feel even more helpless naked. I both wanted and didn't want to know what was going on in the apartment downstairs. I was trembling with fright and morbid curiosity at the same time. A small part of me was pleased because the attack had proved me right: the management refused, out of sheer stinginess, to hire twenty-four-hour guards like in other buildings in the area. The security people are thieves themselves, those neighbors opposed to such extravagance maintain. And isn't that a foregone conclusion? Thieves, that is, folks just like us, people whose goals in life aren't all that different from ours, have opted for other means to the same end, that's all. There's a certain amount of respect in society today for a professional thief: we'd all rather be assaulted by someone who knows what he wants and how to get it.

In the old days, they used to explain vandalism as a form of youthful rage. Not long after the attack, I saw the body of one of the assailants. It was an old man with a long beard and a wooden leg. It's not just gangs of young addicts anymore; there are entire families of vandals, men and women, all different ages. Sometimes the gangs even include children.

The attack was going on in the apartment of my downstairs neighbors, two guys who have lived together for years. Romaris was the name that appeared on the utility bill, and that was the only solid fact I knew about them. You've met them: we used to run into them in the elevator, barely greeting them, and yet they were important; they were among the few acquaintances we had in common; they existed in the tiny intersection of your story and mine. We invented lives for them, relationships, different adventures every day, and all of these seemed to fit in with their rather irregular habits. They were two brothers, a couple of lovers, two old friends, an uncle and his nephew, business partners, dealers in textiles, tinsmiths, antiquarians, trapeze artists, professors.

When the silence returned, I didn't need to turn off the shower to figure it out. It was so powerful that it could be heard over the sound of my speakers blasting at top volume. I opened the door with infinite care. The other neighbors were just beginning to emerge, like turtles peeking out from beneath their shells.

We figured the police would arrive within the next half hour. They do what they can. Just like during a fire or an earthquake, no one dared use the elevator. I went downstairs slowly with the others. The old man's body, filthy, was lying face down in the hallway. A fugitive from a Home? Someone nudged him over with his foot. He had a bullet hole in his forehead, a very small, dark orifice in which a thick, brownish substance, but very little blood, could be seen.

The apartment door was open, obscenely exposing the chaos and destruction inside. Broken glass intermingled with fragments of china and pieces of unrecognizable objects, shoes, combs, and the contents of the trash can, books with pages torn out, and an astonishing quantity of stamps that someone had sprinkled like a merciful snowfall on top of the shipwreck.

They were both there: our downstairs neighbors, our imaginary friends. The big man with the acne-pocked face was dead. It's not that I want to spare you the description of the body; I'm not doing this for you: I'm trying to forget the feeling I got in my stomach when I saw it.

The other one, the younger guy, was looking at the deformed, mutilated body from the depths of such a profound stupor that he seemed not to be in this world. His hand still clutched the weapon he had used against the attackers. He held it in a strange way, as if it were dangerous in itself, not because it was capable of shooting, the way you'd hold a frying pan full of boiling oil.

Each of us is the center of his own universe: one second before yielding to compassion, I felt something like a blow to my chest, the feeling that one of my few witnesses had died. The downstairs neighbors, the ones who had heard our names, the ones who had heard you crying out like a bitch in heat and had smiled almost imperceptibly—at least that's how I'd like to imagine it—whenever we met them on the staircase.

I wanted to run away. Fortunately, the world is full of civic-minded people who are capable of tearing each other apart for the privilege of helping their fellow man. In fact, a couple of neighbor ladies were already vying for the opportunity to calm the weeping man, who had dropped his weapon and was choking on his dry, unbearable sobs.

I went back upstairs feeling vaguely nauseated, with a good excuse to avoid going to the hospital that day, where my father was recovering obscenely fast for a man his age. Very soon they'll operate on him again to connect up his remaining guts and free him of his artificial anus.

I'd been thinking for a while about buying a weapon, and I knew the time had come. When you have a weapon, you need to be prepared to use it; you have to be ready to kill, popular wisdom dictates. The condition of my neighbor's body—his death, in this case, was a mere detail—convinced me that I, too, am capable of using a revolver. In the worst-case scenario, on myself.

You'd be surprised how much I know about weapons. I had to learn a lot for Goransky's film, which had gone through every genre, from romantic comedy to hard-boiled crime drama. I felt confident as I pushed aside the steel gate and entered the gun shop. I had written this scene many times.

"A Sigma," I demanded, unsmiling.

It's a beautiful animal, the Sigma: a stubby, sensible Smith and

Wesson pistol. Just over one-and-a-half pounds, low recoil, adaptable even to a novice's hand like mine.

"Caliber?"

"Nine millimeters, parabellum," I said, with a command of the jargon that concealed my lack of experience.

As the gun salesman explained the advantages of the Sigma in great technical detail, its quick readjustment time after each shot so that the shooter won't miss the target, I absently looked out toward the street. A shabbily dressed man and woman approached the metal grating that protected the reinforced glass door. The man grabbed one of the bars and, without actually shouting, his mouth flew open in a wordless grimace as he was flung backward, landing flat in the middle of the street. The woman ran away. From inside, protected by perfect acoustical isolation, we observed the eerie, silent scene. I spied a video camera peeking out over a balcony.

"It's strange," the gun salesman commented. "Sometimes they're thrown backward, and sometimes they get stuck. You never can tell with such high voltage."

The man noticed my expression and quickly offered clarification.

"Don't worry: whenever a customer comes, I disconnect it. I've never had a problem."

I took the pistol without paying attention to the rest of his comments, although I did agree to try it out, firing a few times at the small target in the shop. I had read so much about its wonderful lightness that its weight took me by surprise. One-and-a-half pounds in a small, compact machine isn't much if you've had previous experience, if you have other sensations to compare it with. For my weapon-innocent hand, this toy weighed plenty.

Once home, I left it on a shelf, close at hand. I don't want to carry it on me. In street killings, the victim can't defend himself unless he's carrying a cocked weapon, ready to shoot. Street attacks depend on the element of surprise: it's always a swift, unexpected act, with no defense possible. That's why prevention is so important: avoiding walking, using armored taxis. Or you can get your own armored car, but that's not for everyone; only people like Goransky can afford that luxury. Every business is responsible for transporting its employees to and from work. Public transportation is scarce, just for those with nothing to lose.

Margot came over that night. We talked about the attack. My story didn't impress her. She had a couple of similar adventures to top mine. Like two patients comparing their ailments, we exchanged anecdotes about assaults and violence.

When the lights went out, Margot was making dinner and telling me about her daughter. Her seduction plan includes an instant family, reinforced by the dazzling quality of her cooking. I myself don't understand why the plan hasn't produced the desired effect. Something always goes wrong; it must be her oppressive, in-your-face style. Suddenly, in the darkness produced by the blackout, we were weirdly illuminated by the gas flame on the stove.

Someone was banging on the door. I didn't get scared: vandals don't knock, and professional thieves don't kill. Just for practice, to acquire efficiency and speed, and maybe to impress Margot, I grabbed the pistol before I opened the door. It was my neighbor, the survivor, the same one I had seen that morning clumsily holding a revolver that he had just used with impeccable precision.

The man was staggering in the doorway, looking at me with unfocused eyes. He had difficulty speaking, as if he had to expel his hoarse voice painfully through a labyrinth of pipes. Nevertheless, he was calm and coherent, as though the horror had affected him only physically. He introduced himself: he was Señor Alberto Romaris, the name that appeared on the utility bill.

He told us that when he arrived at his apartment, the vandals had already been there for quite a while, and there was practically nothing left to destroy. They had no weapons, and they escaped as soon as he started shooting. But it was too late to save his partner. Together, they had owned a stamp and postcard business in a downtown shopping mall. The concierge had mentioned my profession to him, and he wanted to hire me to work on the body, which was going to require more than makeup for the viewing at the wake.

He gave me the name of the funeral home where the deceased awaited me. Luckily, they were people I had worked with before. Some folks get annoyed if the relatives hire a freelancer when they have their own capable, experienced personnel to take care of the makeup and other arrangements.

I remembered what the corpse had looked like: I had felt disgusted and frightened when it was simply some neighbor who had been assassinated by vandals. Now, as a photographic image in the archives of my memory, it seemed almost attractive: an interesting professional challenge.

Romaris seemed dizzy, disoriented. Margot offered to share our dinner with him in the darkness, but he refused. He was wearing the same blue suit I had seen him in that morning, when he'd held the weapon in his hand, but now the suit was stained and wrinkled. He offered me an excessive sum. I thought he'd regret it after a good night's sleep and decided to leave the negotiations for the next day. I volunteered to walk him to his door, which he had reinforced and replaced on its hinges right after the attack.

"Ernesto will walk you to your door; don't worry—I'll lend him to you. You're not well. You need some sleep," Margot told him with that kind attentiveness we use when we want to shake off someone else's pain.

Suddenly the man turned around and grasped my shoulder.

"He wore a retainer," he said. "It really bothered him when he ate, and it hurt him at night, but I made him wear it. I wanted him to have straight teeth."

Then he threw up on my shirt.

So they were a couple after all; you hadn't been mistaken about that. I didn't really have to let him sleep at my house, but the poor guy was frightened, and so was I. More than anything, I felt sorry for him, and he even promised to wash my shirt. I asked Margot to leave; I wanted to hole up in my bedroom and go to sleep.

I pulled out the guest mattress and got Romaris, Alberto, settled in my living room, with a battery-operated lamp. I left him the television in case the power went back on and he couldn't sleep. I thought about using the control chip to block the Suicide Channel but changed my mind: an adult has the right to watch his fellow man commit suicide and even follow suit if he feels so inclined.

I've never thought of killing myself. And yet, at times, when the pain grew so intense that nothing mattered much to me anymore, I did something I had fantasized about ever since I was a kid. One morning at dawn, I lowered myself very carefully six stories down from my apartment, from one fire escape to another, tied to a rope. The next day, my arm joints were swollen and painful, my palms were skinned, and I was bleeding from somewhere near my right armpit, the result of a muscle tear that had hardly bothered me at the time, in the throes of danger and vertigo.

That's how I celebrated your departure. In the turmoil of my grief, a wondrous sensation blossomed: choice. The impossible decision had been between the other man and me. Your husband no longer existed; he didn't count. I always recall that wild descent—feeling the wind, but no fear—as an affirmation of life, a bolt of lightning in the fog that engulfed me.

8

When the morning light returned, my neighbor was still alive to enjoy it. We had a light breakfast together. I promised him I'd go over to the funeral home that very day to examine his friend's body, and I tried to send him on his way, but he wouldn't leave.

He begged me to let him stay one more night. He was afraid to sleep alone. Like a sour, badly digested memory, the image of his apartment and his friend came back to me: broken, stripped, exposed. There was such a panicked expression in Romaris's still-youthful face, with its red eyes and a certain nervous lack of control of the mouth, that I was touched. I imagined the dumb jokes some of my friends, the ones from Zum Zeppelin, for example, would make if they met my temporary houseguest. Since I don't allow myself to feel pity—it's a rich man's vice—I rationalized my decision by telling myself that Señor Romaris was a client: I don't have that many, and I need to take good care of the ones I have.

The man was trembling as if he had a fever. I handed him the thermometer: his temperature was very low. The day before, he had just gone through the motions, numbed by the brutal blow of events: his partner had been murdered; he himself had killed a man. He was still in shock, and the slight tremor he had on awakening appeared to be growing stronger every minute: it moved from his hands to his wrists and forearms, reaching its greatest intensity, like a breaking wave, in his shoulders, which shook uncontrollably. I made him take a muscle relaxant and lie down on my own bed.

My job isn't the kind you do just for money. There was also the pure personal satisfaction, and besides, I was beginning to feel a certain fondness and pity for Romaris; I wanted to achieve something more than just a decent appearance for his friend's body. I wanted to give the poor guy the surprise of seeing his dear departed for the last time with white, even teeth. I was thinking about possible solutions to the broken jaw problem when Goransky phoned. That man lives in his own fictional world, lost in the images of his dreams. His phone calls, when they don't annoy me, make me feel good: they have the ability to remove me from all the undesirable aspects of reality, as if I were receiving a phone call from the future, from some paradise lost or even from some not-too-scary, theater-prop hell, whose flames can be adjusted at will.

Goransky was planning a big party to promote his great film. He spoke to me of the two poles: the Antarctic and the Arctic; of how to reproduce the Aurora Borealis inside an ordinary shed; he talked about great whales; about krill and Eskimos and reporters and distributors and rental hall agents and politicians. I say "Eskimos" even though I know that "Inuit" is the word they use these days, but Eskimos is what we called them in our childhood, and that's the word that still evokes our Western fantasies of ice, seals, and solitude. As usual, Goransky was in an exalted state, in love with his own idea: a big party was exactly what he needed before he started filming. We started discussing his costume and segued immediately into the topic of characterization. He wanted to achieve certain special effects, and he would volunteer not just his own face to my ministrations, but also those of certain very special, very wealthy, extremely important guests: he piled up adjectives, trying to seduce me.

It would have been good news if I hadn't already known my director so well by then: Goransky isn't someone who can look you in the eye and tell you straight out that your job as screenwriter is over, that the magic is gone. He can't do it because he's unable to look at himself in the mirror, look himself straight in the eye and tell himself that his job as director is over, that he'll never make that film in Antarctica no matter how many screenwriters he hires, no matter how many tractor sleds he gets for moving the cameras in the snow he's prepared to buy. I understood he was telling me this, but in a different way. It was no surprise; I expected it. In any case, I appreciated his finesse in firing me by suggesting a new job that would include good contacts, rather than just vanishing without a word.

Before stopping by the funeral home to deal with my new problem, I spent some time at the hospital with Papa. He was recovering, as I told you, almost unpleasantly for someone his age. He was half-propped up in bed when I arrived. At one side was the tray with the remains of the lunch Cora had brought him. While I was there, he stared at his roommate's meal with such intensity that the kid ended up sharing his own dessert with him. Mama clung to Cora's hand like a little girl, staring at my father with ever-renewed astonishment.

When he heard about the attack in my downstairs neighbors' apartment, my father made a sober comparison between my reaction and what he would have done in my place, without ever mentioning the word "coward." Now the anecdote about the wire whip would be inevitable, and in fact, I didn't have to wait long.

When he was very young, Papa lived in the country for a while. An older, stronger man had insulted him, and Papa got even by striking his face with a whip with a wire hook at the end, scarring the man permanently. When I was a boy, this story made quite an impression on me, until I began to notice major discrepancies in it. Sometimes the man was a rural schoolteacher, and other times he was a policeman or a soldier. The events took place either during my father's childhood or his adolescence. The offense alternately consisted of a verbal insult uttered in public, or an unfair deal, or a humiliating order. If, in a particular version, he was still a child, when the moment of revenge came, my father would be lying in wait on a low tree branch, and the man would be riding by on a horse. If, on the other hand, the story took place when my father was already old enough to shave, he would confront his rival on foot, at night, at a crossroads. At other times, the offender would be sitting on a bench with his girlfriend in the town plaza, or else lying with her on the riverbank. The only thing that never varied was the whip with the wire tip and the clean, perfect blow that crossed the villain's face, leaving him scarred for life, like in *Michel Strogoff*.

Despite his apparent well-being, his renewed appetite, and the historic evocation of his righteous anger, when the kinesiologist came and tried to help him out of bed, Papa cried out in pain. His forehead was bathed in a cold sweat.

"He's faking," Cora said. "I know him, doctor. He won't get up because he doesn't want to."

He won't get up because he wants me to lift him, I heard her say wordlessly, because he wants me to offer him my body to lean on, because he wants me to bear his burden again, as usual. But this time he won't be able to count on me, this time he can work things out for himself, Cora said without saying anything, and only I could hear her.

"Listen to me, doctor, make him stand up. He can do it."

The kinesiologist had his doubts, but Cora spoke so convincingly that he finally agreed and, creating a sort of support out of pillows, seated Papa on his horrible wound as the doctor explained the importance of exercising the muscles that support the spinal column. Without his hearing aid, Papa couldn't hear him and just screamed and fought back, if not with all his strength (since he didn't have much left), then with all his weight.

Cora helped the kinesiologist, and between the two of them, they managed to straighten him up on the bed with his legs dangling. Papa gave a terrible sigh, a mixture of death rattle and moan, and fainted dead away. Maybe.

"He's pretending to pass out," Cora explained. "I've seen it lots of times. He always does the same thing whenever he doesn't like something."

Even a stranger would have noted a breath of hatred in the way the words escaped from her mouth, as if she both wanted and didn't want to utter them.

"Old folks have their tricks," the kinesiologist said.

He wasn't all that young himself, and yet he doubted, he doubted. Who can swear he understands the shape and size of someone else's pain?

The only one without doubts was my mother.

"If you ask me, this man is very sick," she said worriedly. "They're letting him die here alone. Shouldn't someone call his family?"

Compared to this scene, the morgue at the funeral home felt like an oasis of perfect bliss.

You never liked it when I talked about my work with corpses. The parties, on the other hand, amused you. Old ladies insisting on stretching their skin as far as it would go, that feeling I sometimes get of applying *fond de teint* on a drum skin. Young women remodeling their already-beautiful features, calculating the possible effects of artificial or natural light, the subtle job of putting makeup on men, as desperate to conceal the makeup as the wrinkles. But you didn't like the corpses, so whenever I thought my conversation was upsetting you, I changed direction. All I wanted was to give you pleasure, since that was the only thing you let me give you. Now, though, I'm not going to let you choose. Without external control, my story can select its own labyrinths.

The manager of the funeral home was an old acquaintance. He helped me remove my neighbor's bluish body, with its tag dangling from the big toe, from the refrigerator. How different a corpse is from the person who lived in that body; it retains just the slightest, vague likeness to what it was in life, a distant family resemblance.

Because of that enormous difference between the living and the dead, which we all would like to minimize, the art of making up corpses is as ancient as humanity. The first, most basic, step must have been the attempt to give the corpse a certain lifelike appearance. To improve that yellowish or bluish tone, which becomes even more obvious when the person has been exposed to sunlight and the patches of tanned, brown, or dull skin contrast with the blue-green shadows under the nose, in the smile lines, or in the bags under the eyes.

For those who can afford the luxury, these parties have changed many customs. Rich people's wakes are like parties, and it's become fashionable to hire artisans like me—some folks call me an artist, but I'm not—who can achieve something superior to a wax doll effect. Now it's not just a lifelike appearance that relatives are looking for, but rather, in many cases, the desire to give their dear departed—even for only a couple of hours—the face he would have wanted to have while alive and that plastic surgeons never quite achieve because they work on living tissue, a substance with a mind of its own.

It's hard to apply makeup to the skin of a corpse. Without a facial expression for support, the flaccid flesh flutters on top of the rigid muscles. It feels like painting on a flimsy cloth draped loosely over a wooden surface. And besides, in this case, I had to struggle with injuries and damages. First I solved the most glaring immediate problems: I repaired the facial bones, closing the open wounds with glue.

Once the most obvious damages are repaired, it's best to work with a photo or a video, combining makeup techniques with others that are almost like plastic surgery and which I permit myself to perform only on cadavers. With living people, sometimes I replace needle and thread with a strong glue that holds the loose skin in place for several hours, allowing me to create Asian-appearing eyes or high cheekbones if I feel like it.

I need to get my hands on the photo or video right away; after a few days, it's hard for relatives to deal with the different faces the deceased used in order to seduce the camera. If you're looking for an ideal face, the one the deceased would have liked to own, the mask he would have chosen to put on before the world, a photo is best: those who know us well are also familiar with our favorite image. On the other hand, if a natural look is what you're after, if you want to recapture the individual, not necessarily as he would have liked to be seen but rather the way others saw him, I prefer to work with a video, a few minutes of the person in action, so different, usually, from the looks that show up frozen in a photo. I look at the images again and again until I myself end up knowing the departed intimately, and without actually having him in front of me, I can work with the corpse until I reconstruct something resembling his living features.

In this case, it didn't take me long to prepare the material, rebuilding the structure of the original face like a painter who prepares his canvas before applying the paint. His teeth would be the hardest part. I stuck the body back in the refrigerator and said goodbye to the manager, who was familiar with my method of working.

I returned home trying to imagine what my life would be like from now on: it's hard for me to envision a world in which my father is dependent on me.

As the elevator rose to the sixth floor, the sound of opera music grew louder and louder. It was coming from my apartment, filling the hallway with unpleasant energy, like the aggressive, antisocial odor of boiled cabbage. I thought about the Suicide Channel, especially that show where suicides, or, rather, their relatives, compete for prizes by showing home videos of sensational deaths: the most spectacular moments are usually accompanied by opera music. Or maybe an interview with the famous transvestite, Sandy Bell, who's clever enough to mix classical culture with the most vulgar popular games.

But the TV was turned off in my apartment. The music was coming from the stereo, and it was designed to accompany an excellent performance by Margot and my downstairs neighbor, Señor Alberto Romaris, on the floor, naked and intense.

I felt happy for the poor guy; extreme pain helps us discover unexpected possibilities in ourselves. Who knows, it might have been his first time with a woman. He seemed to have recovered quite a bit since that morning. They didn't hear me open the door, but Romaris saw me and instantly let go of Margot in a fit of panic.

Margot smiled at me: she had the key to my apartment. She must have run into Romaris as she was letting herself in, and something inspired her to show herself off in a supreme act of seduction: it was clear she had organized the spectacle just for me.

In any event, I thought it wise to turn down the volume.

9

When a woman notices an inexplicable drop in temperature in her relationship with a man, she resorts to jealousy. This inevitably happens, and sometimes it works. However, I'm not so sure anymore that Margot had organized that performance in my honor: even for a man in love, the situation would have turned out more ridiculous than painful. Even a woman as lacking in nuance as Margot would have chosen to let me discover her relationship with another man in a more subtle way.

Did I say I never felt jealous of your husband? I lied, of course. In a way. For long periods of time, I worked things out so I could forget about him: I've always been good at the art of blinding myself to those areas of reality that aren't in my interest to explore. But when, for whatever reason, his existence became intolerably real to me, I felt jealous in every possible sense of the word. For example, that time when you were working long hours every day for some company, keeping a regular schedule, I remember how you insisted we see each other on Fridays and how happy you were that day. "Let's celebrate together," you used to tell me, laughingly. "Free at last!" you would exclaim, referring to the weekend. I didn't share your happiness: I argued that I liked my job, I didn't have a timecard to punch, and Saturdays and Sundays weren't so different for me from the rest of the week.

The truth is, I was hurt by that happiness with which you slipped into our only forbidden days: in so many years of secret meetings, we never spent a weekend together. Two days when you were isolated from me, locked in your world with your friends, your house, your husband, your real life, of which I had no more than a tiny keyhole glimpse. What exactly did you do on Saturdays? Where were you on Sundays? You could have told me about it on Monday, if I had ever decided to ask, but you almost never could have described it to me in advance, on Friday: those were impossible days for me to control or decipher in my imagination because they belonged to a childless couple's world of eternal honeymoon without routine. Like many separated parents, I spent nearly entire weekends with my kids: first as children, and later as teenagers, but always committed to a certain degree of planning, a cherished routine, albeit one you would have found very easy to control.

You never wanted to give me your home phone number. What for, you'd say, I'll call you. Or you can call me at work. And it's true that you called punctually; you never made me wait. Sometimes I could guess it was you by the sound of the ring; we both knew when the other one was calling. Your voice materialized at precisely the moment when I desired, imagined, needed it, and that perfect, invariable harmony, especially on Monday, made me forget your detestable happiness on Friday.

Jealousy. Sometimes I thought I could use it to my advantage. Whenever I was alone, it was incredibly exciting to fantasize about you making love to another man, a faceless man. I tried to turn it into just another game, one of many, to ask you about it and to play at joy and suffering and the sort of desire mixed with violence that only jealousy can create. But outside my fantasy, that faceless man who was part of your reality drove me wild, infuriated me, and my miserable mood ultimately killed my desire. Why did you answer those questions I never should have asked you? Did you think I really wanted to know the last time you made love with your husband? Did you think I was interested in finding out about the games you engaged in? Just because I asked you, did you think I felt like hearing about his style, his foreplay, his most private gestures? Were you punishing me by responding? Did my questions infuriate you and make you choose certain answers in order to torture me? Or did you like participating in that perverse activity I initiated, that chess game for fools that I regretted as soon as I started it and couldn't stop?

Because I didn't want to know that you had been with your husband that same morning, the night before, two weeks ago, or just a few minutes before you came to see me. I wasn't interested in hearing if you did it on the kitchen table, leaning against the wall, in the shower, or in bed. I hated the fact that your words imprinted some arbitrary combination of features that weren't mine on the smooth surface of that faceless man. And you took pleasure in telling me, as if the most attractive part, or, worse yet, the only attractive part, of our relationship was precisely dividing yourself between the two of us, leaving one man so you could see the other one, blending our scents, our sweat, our saliva, and then, instead of inflaming the violent, crazy passion I had imagined I'd feel, your reports would irritate me, stun me, anger me in the worst possible way; I would fall into a sort of frozen self-absorption, an indifference that only masked the pain. Did my anguish amuse you? You comforted me almost maternally, resting my head between your too-firm breasts, breasts that had never nurtured anything but your love affairs and desires, that never had to sag, laden with milk, their weight breaking down the cells that kept them erect.

Your questions were so different from mine. You were genuinely curious about my other affairs, and you interrogated me frequently, nearly every time we met, as if you had to reassure yourself that your impact on my life wasn't completely suffocating, as if you wanted to unburden yourself of the responsibility of making me fall in love with you. I had been separated for only a short time when we met, and although I may have declared my exultation at being free, there must have been the sentimentality of a tango lyric at the heart of my words, the need for a woman beyond sex and desire that you neither wanted nor were able to satisfy. The fact that I pretended to enjoy blissful independence, that I pretended to treat you like just another one of my lovers, balanced out the disparity between our lives; it did us both good.

It wasn't easy. Some of the stories I told you were true; others weren't. The most ridiculous, absurd, or strange ones were that ones that had actually happened. Yet, when I felt the need to invent a romance, I never dared create anything but conventional women, run-of-the-mill affairs, with an attention to plausibility that an alert listener would surely have found suspicious. Ironically, you always doubted—or pretended to doubt—the true stories, and you allowed me the opportunity to embellish details that convinced and amused you. I didn't want to make you suffer, or maybe I did without knowing how. You found everything funnier, more entertaining, than what I had intended; you were too sure of me.

You never did believe the story of my opera singer, for example, but it was true. I left for work in the morning while she was still sleeping, but before leaving, still dazed with sleep, with the dutiful-ness of a well-trained ex-husband, I picked up all the strewn-around clothing, stuck it in a bag, and took it to the laundromat, leaving her in my bed, naked and asleep. I found her just as naked, wide-awake, and furious that night when I returned home very late: I had taken all her clothes, and when she went to throw on some of my things so she could leave, she discovered my habit—you chided me about it many times—of locking the closets. She didn't have a big role in the opera, but it was very important to her; an understudy took over for her in that performance, and she never forgave me for it. We saw each other a few more times after that, but she still hated me.

Whenever I invented stories, though, I stuck to classical, con-ventional professions; I wasn't capable of creating characters more daring than secretaries, dentists, lawyers, or supermarket checkers. More than once Goransky reproached me for my lack of imagina-tion in avoiding hackneyed scenarios, as though I had deliberately tricked him, making him think I was a ingenious, imaginative spin-ner of plots.

Mostly I was an abject failure in my attempt to provoke the same cold anxiety in you that your confessions produced in me (when I think about it, when I really think about it now, how can I be sure they weren't just as fictitious as my own?), describing the racy details, the minute specifics of what happened to me or to those alleged women in bed. I described their scent to you, the color or curliness of their pubic hair, scant or bushy; I compared the sounds that my supposed virtuosity elicited from them, the disconnected words they moaned or murmured at climax, and all I managed to accomplish was to pique your interest, intensify your questioning. You asked me to reproduce on your body the things I'd done or imagined having done to others; you reacted exactly as I had planned to react to your responses, so I got angry again; I could barely contain my exasperation when, instead of sadness or the desire for exclusivity, you revealed nothing more than a repulsive sexual glee.

Don't think I always lied. It was true that I had other women, that they liked me, that I took pleasure in them. And they were all for your sake. Was that really the effect it had on you, or was that just the effect you decided to show me? To deceive yourself in mind and body: isn't that part of loving? It was true, as I said, that I had other women, even when you were with me: you forced me into it. It's also true that I have other women now, but how can I prove that to you? For example, how can I prove to you that Margot exists? How can I prove it to myself?

I said I wasn't sure that Margot had arranged that scene just for me. Now I *am* sure. Now I believe that exhibition of her overripe body, naked and sad in someone else's arms, a man whose dubious virility hardly made him my rival, was designed on purpose—or without a purpose—for my benefit.

Margot isn't subtle, but she nobody's fool, either. She must have noticed my lack of passion, my propriety, that compulsion to complete all the rituals meticulously. Maybe her behavior with Romaris was just an attempt to prove to me that she really exists, a reality she sensed was threatened in my mind.

I think she failed. Margot doesn't exist.

10

One day, a while ago (you had already left, but my kids still lived here), I went to visit my father and found him in bed, propped up against a pillow, sucking on an ice cube. He had had all his teeth pulled. He smiled at me proudly with his wounded gums.

"You think it hurt me? I can stand this and worse. Just look at you," he regarded me scornfully, summing up in a single gesture that mixture of sadness and triumph which my failure—my shabby clothing, my skinny legs, my narrow shoulders—produced in him.

He no longer had his teeth or any way to bring them back, so there was no point getting angry with him. Mama was already a bit absent-minded by then and limited herself to bringing him more ice. But I was furious with Cora.

"You don't give a damn about him! Why did you let him do it?"

"You think he asked my permission?"

In our health system for retirees, dentists collect per capita, that is, for each elderly person registered in their care, whether or not any dental treatment is needed. Therefore, fixing patients' teeth was the last thing any dental professional was interested in: for each job he did, he wasted time and money on materials. My father's dentist had convinced him that he could avoid a lot of pain and suffering by pulling out all his teeth once and for all and replacing them with dentures.

"You'll never find such a cheap set of false teeth anywhere," Papa said to me contentedly.

"You're not going to let him stick that piece of crap in his mouth," I told Cora.

"Why me? Am I any more his child than you are? All false teeth have problems. If I get involved, it'll be my fault. If I leave him alone, we won't have to hear him complain anymore."

She was right. When Papa's mouth healed, his dentist fitted him with a set of enormous, white, perfect false teeth that made him look slightly ridiculous. They gave him a strange resemblance to all the old folks around here with the same kind of dentures, like instant blood brothers.

Just once I heard him complain about his new teeth. We were at a barbecue, and one of my kids asked him what it felt like to eat meat with false teeth.

"Imagine going into a room full of women," Papa said. "All of them beautiful, all eighteen years old, all with their tits sticking out. But you can't take off your gloves."

That's why I loved him; that's why I hated him. Although, under certain circumstances, my father placed money above all else, he was also capable of drinking up life in huge gulps, delighting in it with an infant's absolute egotism. He plunged headfirst into the river of life, while I stood on the shore, worrying and hesitating. Telling myself I was concerned about others, attempting to convince myself of my sense of ethics when maybe I was just afraid.

Right now I can see the image of my father's dentures before me as I search dental supply houses for a suitable prosthesis for my dead client, Romaris's partner. I want something better, more natural, than those fake-looking, too-perfect teeth.

Margot's *mise-en-scène* hasn't affected my professional interest in this task, or even my fondness for Alberto Romaris, who's a little afraid of me, blushing whenever he sees me.

At the time, he had tearfully tried to explain what happened. Whether they were tears of sorrow, shame, or fear, I don't know. After reassuring himself that there would be no violent reaction on my part, he wanted something more: discretion. Not because his friends would look unfavorably upon his relationship with a woman; quite the contrary, that exhibition of new and unexpected erotic possibilities would probably bring him a certain prestige. Rather, it was on account of a sort of superstitious belief (but he'd never tell me that; he'd tell himself) that the rumor might reach the dead man's ears. As if his friend, his lover, his partner might somehow find out, before being buried, that Romaris had been unfaithful to his memory so soon.

I visited several dental supply houses. It wasn't the first time I had looked for dentures for a corpse. In this case, the battering the dead man had received had knocked out most of his teeth. I used tweezers to pull out the remainder of his broken molars, and with a soft plastic, intensely blue paste that had the consistency of chewed gum, I made an impression of his sunken gums. A plaster mold allowed me to make a good replica. I didn't need to custom fit the teeth; corpses don't require comfort. I designed a rather adequate, complete set of dentures, and with the patience of an artisan, working with photographs, I devoted my efforts to reproducing the slight imperfections that would make the dentures resemble the man's real teeth if they hadn't gotten all twisted and ruined. The tiniest tobacco stain here, the hue of old ivory, the canine teeth just a bit darker, slightly crooked incisors. I turned the retracted lips into a gentle smile that would reveal the teeth without drawing attention to them.

Cruelly, with professional pride, I delighted in Romaris's response when he saw the corpse, ready for viewing at the wake. His reaction wasn't unusual. When relatives see my finished work for the first time, they surrender to the most natural impulse: a caress, a kiss, or simply a hand placed on the hand of the corpse. Romaris touched his lover's forehead and, like everyone else, pulled back, startled: there's no way to disguise the texture, the temperature; the feel of a dead man. For the first time, he was able to relax enough to cry for real, with tears, instead of choking on those dry, doggy sobs he gave off when he was at my house. He was quite surprised. He praised my work as much as I had hoped he would, and when he had composed himself, he took several pictures.

Going to the hospital has become part of my daily routine. Yesterday I had a long chat with one of the doctors. Papa has just undergone another operation in which they reconnected the loose sections of his intestine: now he'll be able to control his sphincter. Before, the doctor explained, they used to wait several months between operations. The new, less punishing techniques allow it to be done in a shorter time. In a few days, they'll send him to a Convalescent Home. There he'll have to spend a few weeks in Intermediate Care before he can join the other old folks in their regular activities.

The doctor, a young man, had been seduced by my father's charm and by the unexpected speed with which his incisions were healing. It seemed to disturb him that such a vital person had to go into a Home. But no matter how speedy his recovery, Papa won't be able to get along independently for quite a while. There's no other solution. Now Cora has agreed to put Mama in the Home as well.

"The important thing is for them to be together," she told me, attempting to delude herself with a fantasy she didn't believe. She said it with spiteful pleasure, like someone who's decided to bury a couple of parents in the same tomb, when they had barely been willing to share a blanket.

We finagled a recommendation from the doctor to get the management of the Home to let us visit more often than regulations usually permit. The doctor wrote the note, sincerely moved to discover that, despite our society's harsh rules, even despite legal norms, our family's bonds of affection had developed to such an extent. I noticed his eyes were moist. Perhaps he was thinking of his own father or his own children. Then I realized that Papa had been wiser than all of us. I understood that the dependency he had yoked us with, in which hatred, money, fear, and love intermingled, was much more effective than simple filial affection: indeed, we were detaching ourselves much more easily from my mother, whom we nonetheless loved with a much less contaminated, less complex sort of affection.

Did we love? We *had* loved. Madness is a lot like death.

11

When I was young, many of the classier nursing homes insisted that families turn over the deed to some property—generally the elderly relative's residence—to them as a guarantee of payment. Therefore, from a commercial standpoint, it was to the nursing home's advantage for the patients to die right away. To avoid any foul play that might emerge from this dangerous situation, a law was passed requiring the Homes to dispose of the patients' residences—donation or sale to heirs is prohibited—only while the patients are still alive. Such monies are supplemented by a state subsidy that increases over the duration of the elderly patient's stay, that is, his lifetime. Although the Homes are mandatory for the indigent, too, they're really designed for the middle class: not everyone can make it to old age these days. Not only the families, but the elderly themselves, accept this system. They have confidence in the pleasant atmosphere and the great concern for the patients' health they find in the Homes. I suppose I'm not telling you anything new: wealthier countries were the first to adopt the system, which has spread throughout the developed regions of this inequitable world.

My parents live in one of the nicest neighborhoods in the city, which will soon become a protected zone, in a Home that radiates well-being from the carefully tended front yard on in. There's a marble façade, and a flight of faux stairs leads to the enormous front door, flanked by Corinthian columns. Ramps on either side lead to the small side entryways through which one actually goes in.

The interior is modest, but well cared-for. It's nothing extravagant, but nothing is lacking, either. The Intermediate Care wing, where my father is, smells less of medicine than of perfume: a so-called room deodorizer, intensely floral, floats in the air in the nave; it would remind you of the hotels where we used to meet. When I say "nave," it's not that I'm thinking of a church, but rather because that entire section is designed and decorated like the inside of a yacht. The little round windows, like bull's-eyes, are too small for a body to pass through. This eliminates the need to install window bars. The doors are small and heavy, with huge locks.

You don't see any of those horrors here that the opponents of the Homes used to publicize in photos and videos protesting the law. It doesn't smell of urine or filth; you don't see those piles of rotting garbage that blocked the hallways of the hospital. The walls are pleasantly papered in a bird motif, there are pastel-toned watercolors and wall railings, like barres in a ballet studio, for the old folks to hang onto and cruise along more easily. That detail adds to the impression of a large, solid ship, designed to withstand storms. It's a strange effect for someone who thought he was entering a Greek temple.

They let Mama walk around freely, like the other harmless crazies. It's possible that in time, I'll learn to differentiate between the Parkinson's patients and the ones with Alzheimer's, but at the moment they all seem equally terrifying to me. You don't even have to look at their eyes; you can tell who's mentally ill from a distance, by their posture.

Mama smiles with a blissful expression that makes me feel ill at ease. And then suddenly she looks around, more enraged than frightened.

"They think my house is a hotel," she whispers to me. "But in a hotel, you have to pay! All these people live here, but they don't give me anything, not a cent. They eat and sleep completely free."

We enter the room where my father is, separated from the others because he still needs medical attention. His incisions from the second operation are healing slowly. He looks worse to me, his skin an ugly, sad color. For the first time, there is fear in his eyes. But his familiar, strong voice tries to conceal it.

"You just got here and already you want to escape. You've got a good excuse prepared so you can leave quickly. Go ahead and tell me right now so we won't waste time."

"I'm not in any hurry; I'm staying," I lie.

Why does he have to know everything? And why, especially, does he have to say it?

"Come closer, I want to talk to you."

"Put in your hearing aid; we can't talk if you can't hear."

The hearing aid is on the nightstand. I don't want to get closer and shout into his ear. I don't want to smell his stench of sickness, death, old age, disinfectant, and dried blood.

"Don't think I'm so deaf. You said, 'Put in your hearing aid; we can't talk if you can't hear.'"

"Papa, you're as deaf as a post; I don't want to shout."

"You said, 'Papa, you're as deaf as a post; I don't want to shout.' I can hear you perfectly."

"The stang of the glycenia remures me."

"You said, 'If you don't put in your hearing aid, I'm leaving.' All right, hand it to me."

In a certain sense, that was exactly what I had said. I help him put in the damn hearing aid, which annoys him. I'm beginning to go deaf myself, with very few illusions about it. Hearing aids echo; they whistle; they're uncomfortable.

"Ernie, son, I'm very frightened. Give me your hand; it hurts."

"Your incision hurts?"

"I don't know. It hurts. My spine, my bones. Everything hurts. Come closer, I want to tell you something important. In your ear. But hold my hand tight; that helps."

Mama watches the scene with a curious expression. Forcing him to use the hearing aid has done me no good. Again he's making me lean over and draw closer to his mouth. While Papa speaks into my ear, Mama approaches, takes his other hand, and tugs, trying to pull off his wedding ring. Papa tells me he has a plan to get out of the Home: it'll be easy, Cora already knows about it. He slyly points out the nurse to whom I have to give the money: a young brunette with a hairy mole that disfigures her face. As soon as I feel a little better, Papa says, as soon as I can walk, the two of us will get out of here, and he's not referring to my mother but to me, taking it for granted that I'm locked up with him.

Mama has managed to pull off his wedding ring and hands it to me.

"You read it; you have good eyesight."

I don't have good eyesight, but I don't need to put on my glasses to know what has been written on the ring since forever.

"It's Papa's wedding ring," I tell her. "Here, it has both your names and the date when you got married."

"You read it wrong; it has the day we got engaged. But don't think I'm sad he went away. I'm glad. I threw him out myself this morning; I got tired of putting up with everything, and I told him never to come back."

Mama flashes me her sweetest smile; for the first time in ages, there's an expression of happiness on her face. It must be the medication.

My father isn't prepared to cede control of his possessions while he's still alive. He couldn't prevent the Home from taking his residence, but he's very careful not to let his children get their hands on the rest of the estate. He's right, I suppose. That's why he depends so heavily on our help to get out of here. As is common, the bulk of his money—that fortune which Cora and I imagine, but whose net worth we're unaware of—is hidden from the state's voracity: concealed funds. Only his death certificate in the hands of a certain lawyer will open the keys to the alleged treasure.

A strange, gleeful exclamation interrupts the family reunion. It's a short woman, very heavy from the waist down, wearing not a nurse's uniform, but rather a very form-fitting outfit. Her smile is as deliberately in place as her glasses. She has a large mouth with small teeth, all the same length, as though they had filed down her incisors to avoid a benign, buck-toothed look. Bovine teeth, a cow smile, intelligent eyes.

"How lovely!" the woman says again, more softly. "It's Granny from the fairy tales! How are you, my darling, my sweetheart, my fairy-tale granny?"

And she runs a heavy hand through Mama's white hair. Actually, I hadn't noticed it before, but they've arranged Mama's hair in a tall coil that makes her look like Little Red Riding Hood's grandma. The woman is the manager of the Home.

"And how's my favorite little complainer today?" she asks Papa.

"I want some coffee," Papa says.

The woman looks at me without losing her smile for even one moment.

"Didn't they bring you your Postum?"

"I want coffee!" he insists.

"Coffee is bad for older people."

"In the hospital the doctor let me eat whatever I felt like, whatever my children brought me. Coffee, sugar, salt, real food."

"Here we're going to take much better care of you than in the hospital, darling. They didn't care a bit about you, but we do. Here we won't give you anything that'll harm you."

My father's condition worries me. He seems to have gotten worse in the few days he's been in the Home. I walk out of the room with the manager. I'd like to speak with one of the doctors. The woman realizes my anguish is genuine and removes her smile just as she'd remove her glasses.

"Don't worry, dear, calm down," she reassures me. "We won't let your Papa die here."

And once again she puts on her smile, with its imitation tortoise-shell frame.

12

I have to live as though all this weren't happening. As long as Papa isn't ready to walk yet, it makes no sense to take him out of the Home. I'm trying to forget he exists, even for just a little while.

You'd say that's exactly what I've done all my life, unsuccessfully, tried to forget about my father's existence just as we humans forget death exists, so that we can keep on going as if we were eternal. Don't ridicule me. My father's mocking, scornful smile, superimposed on my memories of you, is quite enough.

And so I've devoted the last few days to business matters, forgetting, or, rather, trying to forget. I contacted some of the new clients Goransky recommended, people who needed help dressing for the Polar Party, which is already being buzzed about in certain circles. For professional as well as personal reasons, I went to Romaris's partner's wake. I wanted to protect my ephemeral creation during its viewing.

At this point, Romaris has become the latest victim of my girlfriend Margot's beneficence. Please, don't let anyone find out about it, he begged me when he was sure I wasn't jealous and didn't hold a grudge against him because of his unexpected relationship with Margot.

Nobody must find out, people say, lumping all their ordinary acquaintances in that category, Nobody. But I knew nothing about that man other than his greenish face under the elevator's fluorescent lighting. Could there possibly have been some mutual Nobody in whom I might have confided? Nobody must find out, Romaris had pleaded, and yet there he was, the day of the wake, gasping with authentic pain and at the same time flaunting Margot to the astonishment and admiration of his friends.

The wake was dignified and modest, nothing at all like a party. On occasion I've done makeup for gay parties, and I had imagined this would be similar. We heterosexuals peek into that world, about which we know very little, about which we have a theoretical and, at best, a well-intentioned conception, with sick, voyeuristic curiosity. That large and (for many) fearsome secret society, whose members don't need to wear a badge or special ID because they recognize one another by looking into each other's eyes.

My fantasy was absurd. A wake is a show with free admission to everyone, including the doorman, the neighbors, distant cousins. Everything was carried out in an atmosphere of extreme discretion.

The deceased's ex-wife and children were on good terms with Romaris. They embraced him affectionately when they arrived. His parents, already approaching that stage of life when it's not prudent to show oneself in public any more than necessary, had nevertheless attended in order to be with him.

The biggest expense was the sandalwood and ebony casket with gold-plated handles, and the food, of exquisite quality. The place was one of those average halls that can be rented for both wakes and parties. It was decorated with real flowers.

There were many people gathered in clusters: relatives, friends, coworkers. Certain faces looked vaguely familiar to me. I recognized some of the couple's friends by sight, from having bumped into them in the lobby or in the elevator. I also said hello to several neighbors from the building. To my surprise, around midnight, Sandy Bell, the famous TV cross-dresser whom no one had ever seen before in men's clothing, arrived. Thanks to hormone treatments and surgical enhancement, only her height and bone structure would make you think she was a man. Although Sandy Bell had never appeared naked, not even in the theater—she flirted at showing off and hiding her body with old-fashioned, feminine modesty—all the news reports made it clear that surgery had added certain artificial attributes without detracting from those with which nature had endowed her. Sandy Bell was an intelligent person, and I had always enjoyed her game and interview show. I was surprised to see her—him?—in person.

I never imagined that our stuffy downstairs neighbors, bureaucrats in suits, would have included her in their circle of friends.

That night at my place, after turning down the music, I had walked away discreetly so Romaris and Margot would have time to compose themselves, get dressed, and leave without making a scene. Since that time I have often chatted with Alberto, but I hadn't seen or spoken to Margot again. I knew we'd run into one another at the ceremony. Margot wouldn't miss a wake for anything in the world.

At that moment, she approached me with the enormous dignity conferred by mourning attire, even when it's merely a question of someone else's mourning. Dressed in delicate gray tones, she very correctly tried to attract the least possible attention to herself. She didn't go anywhere near Romaris unless he called her over. But in fact he called her over pretty often.

"How are your parents?" she asked me.

To assume a worried, compassionate look, she merely had to adjust a few features in her prearranged expression befitting a grieving man's companion.

"That's my business," I replied, tremendously annoyed.

"I know it's your business; that's why I'm interested."

You, who know me so well (or as badly as I know you? I always felt transparent in your eyes, so brilliant at penetrating me but so impenetrable when I tried to look into them), you who know me, I say, would you believe that her ruse worked, after all? If I didn't feel even the vaguest itch of jealousy, not even an annoying little pebble in some corner of my self-esteem, where did those sudden, violent urges come from, that intense desire to slap her for being stupid, for being wretched, for overacting her ridiculous role as the girlfriend of some guy's widower?

Romaris was overcome by a fresh attack of grief every time a new group of people came in, as if each face, each glance reminded him of another facet, another angle of the man he had lived with. Cautiously protecting her discreet starring role, Margot cast glances at the door while talking to me.

I left, confused. Who was I? What did I want? What was I feeling?

What did your absence demolish, what did it leave still standing among my emotional possibilities? What a temptation it was to become a sentimental tango figure, to determine once and for all that life is just an absurd wound.

I felt a desperate need to walk around the city, the real city, not in some shopping center or along a safe, predictable pedestrian walkway. I stopped at my house to pick up my gun. I didn't care very much whether or not it was for self-defense: at that moment, I needed it in an inexplicable way.

In the night sky, tinted reddish by pollution, there were stars. Liquid, quartz lights twinkling against the gigantic screen of the universe. I chose the safest streets, heading steadily downtown. In the daytime you can walk among the crowds in the financial district without serious problems: purse snatchers, robbers, and professional thieves are careful not to make trouble. At night, in the area around the Parliament building, there's plenty of security and few crimes.

I opted for one of the safest ways to walk out in the open: by joining the Mothers' March. You and I and so many others loved and admired the Mothers of the Plaza de Mayo. You'd be horrified to see what this world has done to their proud resistance.

Their Thursday marches around the Plaza de Mayo became an international symbol of the struggle for justice and freedom, and they were so successful that they turned into a sort of pilgrimage destination for those generous, guilt-ridden, overburdened, well-intentioned creatures generally produced by wealthy nations. Over time, the Mothers degenerated into just another tourist attraction, like Bariloche, or Iguazú Falls. Tourist agencies assumed the responsibility of replacing those Mothers who died of illness or old age with substitutes. The marches became a daily, permanent event: they're even included in daytime tours and Buenos Aires at Night excursions, so that even visitors with just a short time to spend in the city can take advantage of them.

The Plaza de Mayo is always surrounded by tour buses. I joined a queue of New Zealanders who had optimistically brought along their white handkerchiefs so that they could take part in the parade. Flashes from their cameras pierced the diffuse, milky light of the Plaza.

I breathed deeply. It was so pleasant to walk outdoors. Inside my pocket, my hand clutched the weapon with unexpected familiarity. Suddenly I was beginning to understand a phenomenon that had always been a mystery to me: what those crazy assassins feel when they burst into a restaurant or a school, machine guns in hand, or what someone feels when he positions himself on a comfortable balcony and kills strangers, using a weapon with a telescopic lens. Suddenly I felt as though the gun was the most logical extension in the world of my own arm, and I knew that if I fired at the queue of tourists, I would feel the discharge precisely like that: like a natural discharge, like the relief you can compare only with peeing vigorously, at length, after hours of holding the liquid in your swollen bladder.

13

A movie director doesn't need to spell everything out or express in words what his images reveal, but I, on the other hand, did need to collect my last payment as a scriptwriter. When Goransky told me about the party and the makeup, I detected a guilty tone of voice that would guarantee me at least a month's pay. I was right.

I went to collect in the morning, at the same hour when we used to have our cheery meetings, hoping he might have left the money with his secretary. I didn't feel like seeing him. I greeted the guards and went into the office without knocking, expecting to find it empty. The vines, so overgrown by now, spread their plump, hairy stems like tentacles, covered with fleshy blossoms whose swollen petals filled the air with a cloying tropical perfume.

I had no desire to see Goransky. Although I knew it was quite possible he would already be working with another writer, what I found still took me by surprise. My replacement, Goransky's new scriptwriter, was a very young girl, quite ugly, frighteningly skinny, with dyed, multicolored hair and an expression of ecstatic admiration that set my nerves on edge. She was talking notes on her laptop, touch-typing so that she wouldn't have to take her eyes off Goransky, who, as usual, was pacing quickly around the room, going up and down the stairs from one level to another, accompanying his diatribe by waving his enormous, hairy arms histrionically.

Just yesterday, or so it seemed, Goransky and I had been together in Antarctica, donning three pairs of woolen socks and thermal under-wear before stuffing our feet into fur-lined boots. We had struggled against the wind and sleet while our breath froze in our nostrils; we had felt that mixture of pleasure and claustrophobia produced by the heat in the common room of the Station, isolated in the middle of the frozen wasteland. Now Goransky was there again: with some-one else.

All the feelings Margot had attempted to arouse in me, that over-flowing, anguished emotion I thought you had taken away forever and that I could no longer feel, suddenly surfaced again. Goransky was at the pinnacle of inspiration; he spoke with clarity, with convic-tion, and above all, with indignant spontaneity. I had heard those same, seductive words, more or less in the same tone, at one of our first meetings.

The girl was as green as I had been: the expression on her ugly little face reflected gratitude to the gods for giving her the oppor-tunity to work with a genius, or at least with a brilliant cinematic talent. In her soulful eyes I could see her certainty that the job was going to be so quick, so easy, just a matter of organizing the ideas that gushed like spring water from Goransky's ingenious mind. She didn't yet realize that the spring would become a stream and then a torrential, turbulent river that would end up sweeping along in its wake the very ideas he was generating, and her own as well, not to mention any possibility of organizing them, pinning them down, turning them into a plausible story.

But it wasn't the imminent, foreseeable problems Goransky's new screenwriter was about to have that worried me. Or the money, either. The stupid truth is that I was crazy with jealousy because he had replaced me, because he believed—although I knew it wasn't true or possible—that another person could do my job better than I could, because Goransky was determined to give it a go with that disheveled, cross-eyed girl who was too young to understand what was expected of her. In a tiny corner of my brain that I tried to hide from myself reared the horrible threat that Goransky and My Rival might actually be capable of inventing that damn story, of writing that damn script and even of filming it.

Goransky stopped in his tracks, embarrassed, as soon as he spot-ted me. He, too, believed he was cheating on me.

"What's the matter, Ernesto? You're sweating," he remarked. My clothes were drenched in sweat. "Is it always so warm this time of year?"

"I don't know. I can't remember. It must be the hole in the ozone layer," I said.

He introduced us. The girl didn't look at me. Did she realize I was acting in a scene she'd soon have to repeat, playing my role? Goransky had the envelope ready with my fee. He handed it to me, walking me to the exit. We didn't discuss the script. What he did was to sketchily describe to me the crazy party with which he intended to attract media interest, and consequently, potential investors in his film. I knew that I needed to save my pity for myself, and yet I felt sorry for that oversized, rich man who seemed like a kid that desperately longs for a toy his parents don't approve of and who doesn't think it's fair he has to pay for it out of his own allowance.

Filming would begin soon, Goransky told me. Now he was sure it wouldn't take long to finish the script, and he wanted to get the journalists interested in it from the first day of filming, following him step by step until the day of the premiere. Nothing like celebrating the grand opening of the project with a huge party. We talked about his own costume and about his wife, who wanted to go as a young Eskimo girl. He also assured me that I had a contract as makeup director for the film. As soon as they started filming, Goransky ranted, I'd have a team of five makeup artists and hair stylists at my disposal, all experienced in special effects.

At that moment, I understood that something worse could have happened between you and me than your simply falling out of love with me, something worse than your falling in love with someone else. Goransky was demoting me from screenwriter to makeup director: it was as if after having me for your lover, you had decided to hire me as a butler. At your side twice a day, passing trays from the left.

But once again I was falling into the trap of false hopes: then, out of passion, now out of spite. I had to remind myself that the film didn't exist, it would never exist, it was just a dream, but the party, however, was real, close at hand, with a date set; they had already begun organizing and financing it. Goransky was in negotiations with several railroad companies, trying to rent Retiro Station. Like those royal parties at Versailles, where the nobility dressed up as shepherds or harlequins, rich people's soirées had a theme. Sometimes the invitation would specify a certain color of clothing; other times, it would suggest that guests come dressed as old-time Hollywood stars. The theme of this party was Coldness, and the costumes were left to discretion of the guests' fantasies. To allow a certain variety in costume, the Arctic and the Antarctic, which was so much more arid, would blend with much less rigor than in the strictly South Pole film Goransky was planning. There would be Seals, Walruses, Whales, Caribou, Arctic Terns, Huskies, Reindeer, bold young lady Penguins and decorous Polar Bear gentlemen of a certain age. The typical creative crowd would come as Igloos, Sleighs, Icebergs, and even Snowstorms. Scholarly types would take the liberty of adopting the arbitrary, fierce guise of the magical spirits, the Tornraks. And the most conservative guests would simply go as Explorers or Eskimos, with stylized costumes designed to withstand heat as well as air conditioning.

Without wanting to, I began to think about my job. I was going to have to study certain effects, the shininess of the grease that the Eskimos smeared on themselves, for example, and I'd need to find out if they painted their faces for religious ceremonies or warfare. It was an interesting challenge: the seriousness of the theme provided few variables. Differentiating between costumes would depend on the ability of the professionals. We would be obliged to work with few colors, subtle tones, the authentic hues of Coldness, looking for differences in tone, shade, and subtleties: black, white, ochre, the entire range of grays, with red reserved for blood.

14

Goransky's party promises to be a source of important work. It's a pity Cora didn't want to help me. It would be good for her to earn a little money.

Too bad you never met her; I wouldn't have to explain so many things to you. Cora has lived sustained by a sort of internal rage that has kept her erect, alert, strong, always ready with a nasty retort, in constant battle with my father. Her movements used to be violent, spastic, like those of a marionette who rebels against the puppeteer's strings, obeying their motion against her will, tugging at them constantly in an attempt to break free. Now that the puppeteer is gone, Cora has fallen to one side of the stage, unable to move by herself.

We had to clear out my parents' apartment to get it ready for the new occupants. As the bureaucratic process unleashed by his stay in the Home progresses, my father's possible escape is looking more and more like a fantasy. Where would he go? The Convalescent Home, with the help of its agency, has already put his apartment up for rent.

Now I better understand other cases I've known, old folks whose children have put them in a Home with the unfulfilled promise that they'll be together soon. Maybe I was too quick to judge them. Besides, the Homes are comfortable, pleasant places. After a certain age, a certain degree of physical impairment, the body is the real prison, and any other confinement is of less consequence.

I've also occasionally heard those rumors about the community of Old Runaways, people who, with or without the help of relatives, succeeded in escaping from the Homes, old folks who were never heard from again, not even a death notice. No one seems to know exactly where or how they survived, but who cares enough to find out? Their relatives don't want trouble. They'd rather act dumb, allowing people to believe their elders died in the Homes and vaguely blaming the mystery on the government or the Homes themselves.

Cora is living with a friend. I was about to suggest that she stay at my place, but I was afraid. People who only know how to obey soon learn to give orders. All her life Cora was subjected to an arbitrary, but rigid, discipline, and she has her own way of doing everything.

Every night before she goes to bed, she leaves her shoes lined up beside the bed so she won't have to escape barefoot in case of fire. She wakes up at 7:00 a.m. and drinks seven cups of *mate* so she can move her bowels. After lunch, she eats half an apple. This innocent habit irritates me because it's so unchangeable. Cora won't hear of any other kind of fruit. And she always eats half, no matter what size the apple is. Now that she's alone, she clings to her habits desperately: they're the only thing she's got left, her reason for being. She's strangely helpless in the face of reality. A middle-aged woman at that point in the road when physical attractiveness is beginning to desert her, one who's never had access to her own money, not even when she was working more regularly.

In one of her sporadic attempts to break free of her chains, Cora studied agronomy. She dreamed of living in the country, but the countryside of her dreams resembled a golf course. Cora would cross the street whenever she saw a large dog; she was afraid of spiders; pollen made her nose run. In the days when the State still tried to cooperate with farmers, Cora worked at the central office of the Institute of Agronomy. When the Institute closed, she couldn't find another job.

For a while, Papa found her a position with one of his clients, an architect who specialized in landscaping mansions. But she thought her salary was a sham, a humiliating sop. Whenever my father assigned Cora a job, simple or complex, it was never a real job, something truly necessary: it was always a way of putting her to the test, an examination she failed before she began.

Clearing out that apartment was a painful task, nauseating at times.

In that slow madness which no one had noticed until it became a full-blown delirium, my mother had amassed all sorts of objects. Mixed among the family photos—those impossibly young faces we couldn't avoid seeing as we loaded them into a box—there were slices of grayish bread, with green mold blossoms and the cottony moss of fungus. In his nightstand, Papa kept an indeterminate quantity of used plastic bags, folded over many times and tied with string from pizza boxes. In the dining room closet, eroded by humidity, a pile of old magazines exuded an odor of wet, abandoned paper. In the bathroom cabinet were dirty stockings, clothespins, curlers entwined with strands of hair, combs with broken teeth, rusty hairpins, lots of small soap fragments, and what seemed to be an infinite number of leftover prescription bottles. And underneath a loose floor tile, the famous ledger with Papa's notes. At a first, cursory glance, we found the numbers and letters incomprehensible. I gave it to Cora. When it became necessary, we would sit down patiently and decipher it.

My parents had traveled a great deal and enjoyed it, and had accumulated amusing little objects in glass cases, souvenirs of the countries or cities where they had been momentarily happy. With that infantile gaze we children never lose completely where our parents are concerned, Cora and I imagined that those untouchable decorations—Mama was the only one authorized to clean them, with a rag dipped in alcohol—made of porcelain, crystal, ivory, veined jade, ebony and aromatic wood, were valuable curiosities. But with its owners far removed from the scene, the entire house revealed only its grief and pain to us: the disconnected toilet in the master bathroom, the kitchen faucet tied with a rag, the oven door held on with wire, the dirty, worn-out paint on the walls that we saw for the first time with objective eyes.

We looked over the knickknacks one by one, trying to decide which were worth keeping and which we would leave behind. The glass bear was cloudy on the inside; the clown had a broken arm; some paint had chipped off the shepherdess and her dog; the set of painted plates wasn't porcelain but rather cheap ceramic; everything that wasn't made of plastic was broken, scratched, chipped, or faded from the sun. Sadly, I realized there was nothing, absolutely nothing there that I might want to keep, except maybe that naked, reclining woman, whose oversized breasts were salt and pepper shakers and which struck me as the most touching symbol of my father's bad taste and his enthusiastic vitality. But I would have been ashamed to take it in front of Cora.

"How did they end up with all this?" I asked, horrified, as we removed a strange collection of plum pits and watermelon seeds and various bits of more or less unrecognizable broken objects from my mother's closet: an old, gutted telephone; pieces of an enormous, ancient office calculator; some unidentifiable item with wires and gears.

"How should I know? You live in a place and you just don't see it; you forget, you get used to it little by little. And what about you? You're an outsider—how come you never noticed?"

I didn't answer her. I kept searching. As I tried to create an illusion of order out of the chaos in which we were buried, as I piled the forty-two thick and thin sweaters to one side (all different colors, all moth-eaten, with frayed elbows), as I attempted to separate the relatively important documents from the miscellaneous papers that filled the drawers, I searched, searched frantically, without realizing it. We had planned to classify the objects: we put those that were just garbage on the floor; those that could be sold, exchanged, or given away on the table; those we wanted to keep, on the double bed. Mama's Persian lamb stole with its little mink collar, my father's old camel's hair overcoat, were spread out on the bed along with two dozen place settings stolen from different airlines. On the floor, in monumental disorder, were heaped: a scratched rolling pin; several different-sized metal colanders, rusted and in various stages of disrepair; cloth remnants so old they fell apart at a touch; absolutely ruined garments. Cora and I couldn't agree about anything, and we constantly picked up and laid down articles of clothing or piles of newspapers from the big table. And I kept searching.

Much later, when I was alone, I understood. I was searching for something more, a secret, proof or evidence of something else, an unknown story that might help me comprehend more clearly, that might give new meaning to my father's life, as though his public image, the face and form he displayed before us, weren't enough. I needed to know more about him, about his desires, his thoughts, his ghosts, something beyond the mask he put on for the world. I searched among the remnants, among the traces of his life, for proof that he, too, was human, inconsequential, weak, proof that he had once had a moment of madness or passion, something that might reveal more than the constant calculation, the cold assessment of monetary worth, the cost of production, the sale and resale value of everything in this world. I was searching for you. Once again, as always, I was searching for something or someone that could have meant to my father what you meant to me: something absurd, unsuitable, a crack. I found nothing. I'm sorry.

"Papa told me about his plan to escape. I guess you're okay with it," I said to Cora.

"Why can't you ever understand anything? You're always so detached," Cora said.

Suddenly, she became enraged. Her cheeks flushed. It might have been one of the objects we found, which she saw in a new light in that house where she had lived for so many years, or maybe it wasn't any one thing in particular but simply the mere accumulation, that precipitated a burst of adrenaline and passion in her.

"To make a long story short, I do your share of the chores. I go here, go there, I put up with it. Now Papa's pretending to be dying, and he wants to drive me crazy in the process."

"You want a *café con leche?* I'll make it for you. With lots of foam," I replied.

That's how it's always been, ever since we were kids: a *café con leche* was the only thing Cora would accept from me. It had the strange power of calming her, making her see things my way, turning her hateful words, which always seemed jumbled because they emanated from an internal, incommunicable horror, into coherent speech.

I found coffee, sugar, and a container of powdered milk. Cora went to wash her face and hands. The grime that flaked off everything made our noses itch and stuck to our fingertips, embedding itself in our fingerprints.

We drank our *café con leche* in the kitchen.

"Now he's acting like he's the offended party," Cora insisted. "He can't stand it when Mama goes near him, but the nurses comb her hair, put rouge on her, and send her to him anyway. They think it's sweet to see two old people together for so many years. You should see the way he curses her out. He always acts like he's the one who's hurt, but he can't fool me anymore."

When we were teenagers, Papa used to steal Cora's wallet from her purse to show her how careless she was. She would leave the house with the bus fare in her hand, without checking to see if she had her wallet, and suddenly, when she was ready to go home, she would find herself in the street, far away, without a cent, without her papers. And she knew he was responsible: no one else could have stolen her wallet so cleverly.

"What hurts him?" I asked. "Is it the incision?"

"How should I know if it's the incision? His stomach, his bones. He can't find a comfortable position."

"Are they giving him pain killers?"

"They've got to give him something, right? I don't think he needs a pain killer. What he wants is for me to be there night and day, that's all. Luckily, they don't allow visitors all the time."

"But weren't you going there a lot?"

"They don't allow it, but I bribed the guard at the entrance, and I made a deal with the nurses. I was going night and day; he can't be left alone. But he can't fool me—nothing hurts him, it's a lie. Don't you think I, of all people, can tell when his complaints are real?"

In the days when Cora was working and lived alone, Papa phoned her every day at six-thirty in the morning so she wouldn't oversleep. Once, when Cora answered the phone, she could hear horrible moans, something like sobbing or screaming at the other end, the death cries of a tortured baby, the strangulated voice of someone who's been mortally wounded and is trying urgently to communicate a desperate message that he can't manage to articulate. At first, the wake-up call was so frightening that Cora, terrified, after trying to elicit a clearer message, ended up adding her own screams of horror to those coming from the other end of the line. After a while, Papa called back, laughing: that was his idea of a joke. After that first time, Cora no longer got scared. She left the phone off the hook. But she knew that as soon as she hung up—not always, not at any specific hour, not every day, but at any random moment, at any time of day or night—she would be the target of Papa's jokes, which included, in addition to the ever-changing cries, panting and threats in a whispered, disguised voice. It was to remind her of the dangers of living alone, Papa said, so she would always be alert, so she wouldn't open the door to strangers.

"But how do you know he's faking?" I asked her.

Papa had looked pretty sick to me the last time I was with him. That skin tone, that cold sweat, weren't easy to fake.

"Nothing hurts Papa because he's incapable of hurting! Don't you realize he doesn't feel anything?"

"Then he's okay to leave."

"Are you crazy? He's very sick! What are we supposed to do with him? Where will we hide him? We'd have to build him a hospital with round-the-clock nurses, strong people who can move him. He's still big and heavy."

"Did you talk to the nurse or didn't you?"

"I talked to the manager of the Home. She's a very intelligent, perceptive person. Her own mother was a patient. She understands our situation. And she agrees with me that nothing hurts him. She figured Papa out right away."

I remembered those tortoiseshell glasses and that bovine smile, her small teeth, her intolerable perkiness.

"Then they don't give him pain killers?"

"Yes, they give them to him anyway, even though they know he's faking. You can't give just anything to old people. The manager told me all about the problem of side effects."

15

I used to like arguing with you. I liked your futile passion, and sometimes I provoked it. That was our pact: the passion, the emotional outbursts, were up to you; I was supposed to provide a certain amused indifference, a calm in the intellectual swordplay that allowed me to gaze at your exposed loins and might have led me to the final thrust if it hadn't been for a sudden, deft twist in the discussion. Your enthusiasm launched the verbal swords into the air, and the duel became a wrestling match that you always won.

For example, you used to talk about women's rights, about women's triumphant assumption of power, and I deliberately reminded you, just to annoy you, of the painful effects this new development was producing in our society. I pointed out—with seamless reasoning—that for centuries women had taken care of children, the elderly, and the sick, all of whom are now entrusted to the care of institutions: nurseries, Homes, hospitals. And since those institutions employ females—underpaid workers—women are still taking care of children, the elderly, and the sick; but instead of their own dependents, they have to look after strangers, other people's dependents, as if they loved them.

You became furious when you couldn't shoot down my arguments. How I loved you then—tousled, angry, and naked! I was the one responsible for the flush in your cheeks; you belonged to me a little more. I really loved making you mad.

Now I can't get that argument out of my mind. I've just been to the Home; I'm writing so I can forget what I saw, and also so I'll never forget it.

On Sunday, the official visiting day, after stopping by my father's room, Mama, Cora, and I had tea in the dining room of the Home. There were other visitors, but not too many, especially not for the newer arrivals. You should see how lovely, how pleasant, that place is. A skilled decorator chose blond wooden furniture, synthetic, ivory-toned prints, imitation Thonet chairs with armrests to help the old folks get up more easily. On the walls hang large paintings, reproductions of such familiar, such infinitely reproduced Old Masters, that they've lost their original, offensive power and have become just subtle, refined decorations.

The waitresses, dressed like Dutch peasant girls with wooden shoes and bonnets (I imagine not all Homes are like that: I suspect it was one of our manager's fantasies; she looks like someone who loves tulips, those profuse, predictable flowers), served tea, coffee, toast, cookies, and jam to the old folks and their visitors. It was a large room, filled with people, and the first thing you heard was the silence.

The old people didn't talk. Some of them were much younger than Papa, but they all had the same tormented, lost expression. The liveliest ones concentrated on consuming what they had been served. The few visitors from the outside world didn't seem like they could find topics of conversation that would interest the patients, although some were chatting with them very quietly. If two old people happened to be sitting at the same table, they didn't even look at each other. That concept of camaraderie which might be established among the patients, those friendships or grudges you see in movies, were relegated to just that: a movie concept. Deaf, isolated, and in the majority of cases with serious mental problems, the residents didn't seem to have any interest in communicating among themselves.

Mama was sitting between Cora and me. The coffee was Postum, the tea tasted like piss, and I couldn't identify what the bread and cookies were made of, but it was obvious, just as the manager had threatened, that there was nothing harmful there. It was a question of proper nutrition: fiber and subsistence. Aside from the bedrooms, the dining room was the only place where the patients could meet with their relatives; they had also wheeled in a few old folks connected to their nasogastric tubes. Planted in wheelchairs, they couldn't have spoken if they'd wanted to, but their vacant stares betrayed no desire to communicate.

"I thought the old folks interacted more with one another," Cora remarked to the waitress who brought us the tea. "Like playing cards, for instance."

"Aren't they adorable?" the waitress asked, rhetorically, casting a glance around. "Sometimes we make them play cards, when we have time. You have to put the cards in their hands and help them to throw them on the table. It's a lot of work."

We had just come from seeing my father, and I thanked God for getting me out of that room while feeling miserable for escaping. I sat precariously on the edge of the chair, unable to decide whether my next move would be to skip out while I still could or to run right back to Papa's side.

Mama was quite calm. She had sunk into an indifferent torpor that appeared to be medically induced. A purplish, swollen bruise disfigured her nose. According to the nurses, she had fallen trying to climb on a chair to reach something on a very high shelf, something only she could see: she had fumbled in the air, looking for Papa's hat, with the idea that no one could get very far without a hat. The story was plausible, but still I was suspicious. How could I be sure they hadn't struck her? Her exaggerated calm made me think they had given her sedatives to keep her under control. She had momentarily lost the most flagrant symptoms of her madness. She didn't talk to us about secret messages; she didn't seem to be hallucinating; she had even recognized us with a sort of bored resignation. Her answers were coherent but lacking all emotional tone. Her clumsy hands could barely grasp the cup handle, and she chose a piece of bread because she couldn't pick up the dainty cookies. In addition to her arthritis, a long-standing problem, she seemed to have lost her fine motor coordination. A white sediment of dried saliva clung to the corners of her mouth. Her speech was slurred, as though she had difficulty manipulating her tongue.

Cora regarded her happily, with a good-natured smile.

"Did you notice how well Mama seems today?"

"It scares me."

"You're scared because you're so egotistical; can't you see she's not suffering?"

"I brought you some candy," I said to Mama, practically whispering in her ear. Cora got angry.

"You know that's not allowed! Sugar is bad for her."

I tried to sneak the filled candies to Mama under the table, but she didn't seem interested; she didn't make the slightest effort to take them or to reject them. It seemed our visit was annoying or boring her.

Suddenly, something horrible happened. At Cora's insistence on the importance of good nutrition, Mama took a big swig of pseudo-coffee with milk. But, as if she had suddenly forgotten the sequence of movements necessary for swallowing, she sat there with the liquid in her mouth, like a little kid who refuses to eat.

"Swallow, Mama," Cora said.

"Spit, spit it in here," I said, holding out an empty cup.

"It's better if she swallows it," Cora insisted.

"It doesn't matter; what's important is that she get it out of her mouth," I said. "Spit it out, Mama."

"Come on, Mama dear, down the hatch!" Cora said.

"You don't have to drink it if you don't like it," I said.

But Mama appeared to be frozen in an eternal moment, with her puffed-up cheeks and her mouth full of liquid. A few drops escaped her tightly sealed lips, running down her chin. She looked at us with desperate eyes, but her anguish seemed to have no relationship to what was happening to her. She could neither spit nor swallow, and it seemed like she would stay that way forever, for hours and hours, with her mouth eternally, agonizingly full.

We called for help. I fantasized that the nurse would throw a violent, two-fisted punch at her swollen cheeks. That was what I feared, maybe because I myself felt the same temptation to strike her that way, like someone exploding a paper bag he had just blown up. But the nurse just stroked her hair gently and brought her a plastic bib-like thing with Velcro at the neck, like the ones they use in barber shops to protect clothing.

"Sometimes they stay that way for up to two hours," she told us. "You have to be very patient. Eventually it all comes out. It's impossible to pry their jaws open; you should see how strong they still are."

In our desperation not to be left alone with that wrinkled doll who had been our mother, like a poorly ironed, yellowish rag with desperate eyes, we asked the nurse questions in order to keep her with us a little longer: two minutes, five minutes, fifteen minutes more.

You'll probably think this is atrocious, but tolerating that torment struck me as a reasonable price to pay—I was making a deal with destiny—to avoid returning to the room where my father was groaning in pain.

For the first time ever, Papa let me in without reprimanding me, without making harsh comments, without feigning indifference or joy.

"Son," he articulated with difficulty, the words forming part of a deep sigh, "don't leave me."

Against his grayish pallor, the circles under his eyes stood out like dark stains. He was trembling. He moaned constantly, almost involuntarily, as if the air coming from his lungs made his vocal cords vibrate more than he wanted them to. I felt afraid.

"What hurts you, Papa?"

"Everything. My bones. A shot. Please, make them give me a shot. Please."

He wasn't making cynical jokes; he wasn't complaining about the food or how the nurses were treating him. He was just lying there, engulfed in pain, sinking into a swamp that refused to swallow him up completely.

"Ask the nurse. Offer her money. Make her give me a shot," he begged.

I looked at Cora, who shook her head incredulously.

"He thinks his money can accomplish everything. If he doesn't need a shot, they won't give it to him. They're strict here."

"But can't you see he's about to explode with pain?"

"He's faking."

Papa looked exhausted. He fell asleep for a moment. His breathing slowed, but he continued moaning in his sleep, without a pause, without a respite, without losing the rhythm.

"You're crazy, Cora. Don't you see he's even moaning in his sleep?"

"He even fakes it in his sleep. Well, in a manner of speaking. It's mechanical—can't you tell by the rhythm? It's not from pain; it's a mechanical effect of his breathing, something he's got in his trachea."

Papa opened his terrified eyes and began panting, as though he were in excruciating pain. When my wife was about to give birth to our first child, she went to a class where they taught her to pant. After giving birth, she laughed about it: as if panting were voluntary, she said. As if you could do anything else but pant when the pain comes and traps you and digs its nails into you.

But my father's panting was over quickly, and his body, sprawled out on the bed, began to emit those long, empty, painful wails.

I called for a nurse and asked her to give him a pain killer. She brought a pill and a glass of water. She lifted his head to help him swallow. My father kept begging for a shot with an anguish that transcended all reason.

"I'm going to look for a doctor," I told Cora.

"Do whatever you want," Cora replied. "It's obvious you don't come here every day."

When the doctor arrived, my father stopped being a suffering piece of flesh for a moment, and his face took on a human expression.

"Give me something, doctor. I'm an old man. I don't want to suffer. You're an older man yourself—save me. Take away the pain. Give me a shot."

The doctor seemed very self-possessed, immersed in his role, an actor who had played the same part for many years, always receiving the same applause from very diverse audiences.

"Señor Kollody," he told him, reading his name on the chart, "we've given you a strong sedative. The oral form takes a while to work, but it's just as effective."

I couldn't tell if my father hadn't heard him or if he simply didn't want to listen.

"You can do something to make them give me a shot."

"For God's sake," I said to the doctor quietly, "give him a shot, anything at all, water, glucose, whatever!"

"Don't interfere," Cora said. "The doctor knows what he's doing. Trust somebody for once in your life!"

"The pill you took will help you, Señor Kollody," the doctor told my father. "You have to believe me, that's the important thing."

"I believe you, doctor. Put your hand on my forehead. Like that. Stay with me for a minute. If you're here, I feel better; I need you."

Papa's attempt at seduction was fruitless. The doctor seemed more rushed than touched. As soon as he managed to disentangle himself from my father, he said goodbye and left.

"Get me out of here, please, for the love of God, get me out of here. I still have a chance if you get me out of here," Papa said, before plunging into pain once more.

"We'll talk later," Cora said. "Now we're going to have tea with Mama. You haven't been to the dining room yet—you'll see how lovely it is."

16

We makeup artists, like plastic surgeons or photographers, work on the most delicate area of the human form: we work on the living flesh of vanity. When I first pretended to be a makeup artist in order to help out a friend—a photographer who wanted to impress his clients by showing off his nonexistent team of associates—I didn't envision that this would someday be my principal occupation. Above all, I didn't imagine that it would become a vocation.

I enjoy giving people the gratification of seeing themselves look more like their ideal image for a while. The expression of joy on my clients' faces when they look in the mirror is part of my own happiness. I feel like an author who takes pleasure in the laughter or tears of his readers. Sometimes, though, the opposite happens: disappointment or horror. Any one of my colleagues can tell you about the rage—the pain—of men and women whose mirror doesn't reflect the image they intended to achieve. Disappointment is more frequent among men, although they show it less, because women are better acquainted with what makeup can and cannot do, while men imagine that a good dye job on gray hair, a deft touch with wrinkles, will give them back the appearance and impatient virility they had at twenty. Some, those who aren't able to sustain the mystery of a glance, become suddenly ridiculous, like grotesque old scarecrows; they get mad or sad, and they always hate you.

That's why, when I work for new clients, and especially for a party, I insist on practice sessions. I want to know the person whose face I'm about to submit to my imagination, my hands; I need to have a long chat with him, understand his desires, which generally defy simple characterization. You have to practice, come to an understanding, make sure there won't be any last-minute surprises, like when half an hour before the party, the man or woman discovers that they can't stand that startled, angry face they see in the mirror or realize that they simply expected something else.

Goransky's wife, for example, doesn't want to be just an Eskimo girl; she wants to be an Eskimo girl with violet eyes, like a certain famous actress. I was working with her, with her face, her personality, studying her a bit so that I could determine how far she could delude herself, to what extent she could help me make her believe she had begun to resemble that woman, once considered to be the most beautiful woman in the world, but since (luckily for me) the actress hadn't died in the flower of her youth but rather had followed a downward path toward deterioration, growing ungracefully fat and old, a long series of images superimposed themselves on that perfect image my client dreamed of, making it less precise, more imperfect.

And the entire time I attempted to transform that older woman, who probably hadn't even been beautiful as an adolescent, into a young Eskimo girl with violet eyes, I saw my father's face reflected in the mirror.

Very few of my colleagues, only the youngest, boldest ones, choose to work without a mirror, hiding the slow, unpleasant stages of the metamorphosis, risking it all on the final effect, the client's happy surprise as he looks at himself as if for the first time. Experience teaches us to avoid that risk; it's better for the person to see himself deliberately made unattractive, his hair covered with a towel, distorted by the lack of shadows and nuances created by a very thick base coat. It's preferable for him to have control over the progressive reappearance of life, an artificial life recreated in the face we began working on, deliberately transforming it into the smooth, inexpressive mask of a statue.

The first thing I did in Soledad Goransky's case was, as usual, to cover the scar lines caused by facelifts at the edges of her face, especially above her forehead, almost at the hairline. They're very fine, white, shiny lines. The most practical approach is to cover them with liner slightly darker than the skin. Though it seems illogical, it's easier to make a dark line disappear than a light one under makeup base. With the hair combed forward in artfully uneven bangs, you can cover up the obvious secret that doesn't want to be revealed.

Clients expect a makeup artist to be either a woman or gay. It's not a prejudice; it's an opinion based on experience. Most of my colleagues are. Painting one's face as well as other people's is a job that for centuries was considered so feminine that many feminists refused to do it. My clients—both men and women—feel uncomfortable when they discover or suspect that my proclivities are different from those of the average person in this profession. Soledad Goransky noticed it right away. I thought she seemed uneasy beneath my hands, which were working on her face, covering it with successive layers of makeup: moisturizing cream; pencil to conceal scars; base color, a little darker here, a little lighter there, to modify her oval-shaped face, accentuate her cheekbones, disguise her double chin, make her nose appear thinner; a thicker base coat to cover her skin, still firm, but ravaged by facelifts; an invisible powder to tone down shininess in some areas and add deliberate shine in others; powdered blusher to brighten the entire face.

I didn't want to mention the screenplay from which I had been excluded; the blow still hurt me. I chose to ask her about the party instead.

She described the complicated negotiations that allowed them to rent one of the main municipal train stations, converting it into a reception hall for a few days. Although the Goranksy home is grand enough to seduce investors and entertain TV producers, these days it's become fashionable to rent a place customarily used for other purposes—a factory, a warehouse, a seized house, a sanatorium, a bank—and turn it into a sumptuous Party Palace, before returning it to its rightful owners and its normal activity. It's a ridiculous affectation, outrageously expensive. When you rent a location where services are provided, you have to compensate the customers; when you rent a house that's been taken over, it costs quite a bit to evict the tenants, even temporarily, as they fear losing a roof over their heads forever.

That outrageous expense, apparently senseless, coincides with the special significance of parties: gigantic displays of power.

But while I chatted about other subjects, with one corner of my mind focused on the required steps of my job, which experience allowed me to exercise mechanically, I kept seeing the image of my father, tethered to his pain. The central portion of my mind reviewed various alternatives, fluctuating between extremes: from taking Papa out of the Home, no matter how, taking charge of him, fighting to save him, to forgetting the whole business and opting for what most people would do: not going back to see him — for days, years — until they called me to notify me of his death. Ultimately, I couldn't avoid leading the conversation toward the crux of my obsession.

"Is he in a hospital or a Home?" Soledad was a tall, strong woman, a good person; there was something trustworthy about her that allowed me to talk openly.

"A Home. A good one, apparently," I told her, relieved to be able to discuss the subject with someone besides Cora.

"They're all good. If he's in a Home, you don't need to worry. He's in no danger."

"Are you speaking from personal experience?"

"In a way. We have investments in Homes; they're quite profitable. Hospitals are dangerous because they require a rapid turnover. But if they accepted him in a Home, it's because he's going to last: they can tell; they're very well run."

All that day I visited clients, trying to deaden myself through work. The temperature outside was very high. The blast of hot air that hit me when I went from one air-conditioned area to another raised the hairs on my arms. I attempted to make up a very fat man in a place where the air conditioning wasn't working, but I had to give up; the relentless moisture on his skin prevented me from applying color. I had set up one appointment after another, so I was compelled to listen to other people's voices, to pay attention to their words. At the same time, all day long I heard my father's moans. I couldn't escape; I was as trapped as he was. I forced myself not to return to the Home. I knew Cora was there, at his bedside, insulting him and trying to make him eat some chicken soup.

At night I tried to write to you, but I was too miserable to concentrate on the screen. Surprised by my own impulse, I went downstairs to ring Romaris's doorbell, hoping he'd be alone—I didn't mind running into one of his friends, but for the love of God, I didn't want to see Margot—and we ended up getting drunk together. He offered me a joint, too, but I was afraid the marijuana would make me feel even more wretched.

The heat took up all the available space, and we both had trouble breathing. At first we couldn't avoid awkwardly discussing the false spring that had invaded the city, but soon we began to compare memories, trying to decide if it was true that in the old days, the temperature didn't climb so quickly in this part of the universe. Although he's younger than I am, we soon found ourselves sharing bits of memories for no particular reason. I showed him pictures of my kids; I told him about the e-mails I received from different parts of the world, the frequent, trivial chats, until I worked myself up into longing for those terribly old-fashioned, forgotten long-distance calls of my childhood, infrequent, expensive, difficult, where garbled voices acquired an importance that was magnified by the cost per minute.

He returned my confidences by describing his partner's kids with enormous tenderness; he imagined he would have loved one of his own children in the same way. He was wrong, of course, but why tell him that? Although I didn't ask, he mentioned that he hadn't seen Margot again since the wake. They had parted on good terms, affectionately, but with the clear understanding that neither of them wanted a repeat encounter.

So many times you and I wondered what our downstairs neighbors' lives were like, those two gentlemen of different ages, so alike in the way they dressed, always gray suits, shirts with cufflinks, patent leather shoes, the same quick, courteous gait. I didn't find much to object to in Alberto Romaris's apartment: an imitation Bauhaus chair; a lightweight table, delicately supported by a central leg, like a wineglass and yet somehow solid; good chairs that took your backside and its alignment with your spine into account, in addition to having a certain visual effect.

As we talked and drank, I wondered why I felt so comfortable with a man who was so different from me, how it was possible for someone my age to discover a kind of friendship that followed a different path. I'm aware that I'm exploring certain limits here, and I assure you that I questioned myself candidly in order to unearth some kind of sexual interest in poor Alberto—to no avail. Maybe I was just looking for a crack in our conversation, an excuse, a refuge, so that I could talk about you, could ask him if he remembered you, if he remembered us.

You never met my friends, no one who had anything to do with me. Your precautions drove me crazy. But who knows if I would have desired you so, for so long, had it been otherwise. Our relationship could have evolved into tenderness, into habit, into love, but thanks to your strict notions of secrecy, it always stayed the same, miraculously sustained by desire through the years.

I live like an old bachelor these days. The Monday meetings, for instance: that diverse group of men who meet for dinner once a week at the Zeppelin. Some of them know each other from work; others are friends of the founders and met there for the first time. I'm not one of the regulars; it's too expensive to go every week, and the need to keep up with the old adolescent games—the constant physical and verbal sexual humor, the bragging, the hidden power plays, that typical male need to establish hierarchies—it all wears me out.

In spite of the strange episode with Margot, that kind of confrontation was missing from the relationship I was beginning to establish with Romaris. In any case, I think it's something like the friendship a man forms with a woman he doesn't desire, even though she may want him.

17

I didn't want to go back to the Home. I don't need to give you too many explanations: I'm a coward. If I weren't, I never would have agreed to share you.

We fearful men are like babies who cover their faces to hide themselves: what we can't see doesn't exist, isn't threatening. I didn't want to see my father's suffering again.

But I had no choice.

I entered through a side door. I greeted the guard, mentioning Cora's name. It's the entrance she uses every weekday, when visits are forbidden. From there, you can go directly to the Intermediate Care area without having to cross through the entire Home.

Inside, it was nice and cool, as usual. Overcoming all other sensations, the air conditioning made me sigh with pure physical pleasure.

The nurse who was changing Papa's IV wasn't startled; it was as if the presence of family members were an unusual, although not unforeseeable, fact.

"A very strong guy, your dad. We had to restrain him so he wouldn't pull everything out," she told me. "Since you're here, help me change the syringe; this vein's all used up."

One of Papa's legs trembled convulsively beneath the sheets. His swollen belly rose and fell irregularly to the rhythm of his agonized breathing.

"Don't let her," he said, looking me directly in the eye. "Please don't let her stick that needle into me again. Please."

"Is it necessary?" I asked. "Isn't there any other way?"

"The patient isn't eating. He's not going to get well like this. The IV keeps him hydrated."

I squeezed his bound hand firmly while the nurse searched for a vein. Papa let out a horrible scream. The nurse inserted the needle on the first try, secured it with tape, and adjusted the bag. It seemed to me that everything happened very quickly, but my father kept screaming.

"That's all; I'm done now, Señor Kollody."

From the volume of her voice, it was obvious that the nurse knew him, or maybe she was just used to the fact that all old people are more or less hard of hearing.

But still my father screamed; he howled wordlessly, and I squeezed his hand; I squeezed it harder and harder, until, his mouth all dried out with fear and pain, his speech impeded by the absence of his false teeth, he managed to control his screaming enough to make himself understood.

"My hand!" my father whimpered horribly. "You're breaking my hand!"

I let go, horrified.

At that moment, the door suddenly opened, and, like a sudden, icy gust of wind, the manager of the Home walked in. She had come down the hall running, and she was panting without dropping her smile.

"Señor Kollody, I've told you not to scream. You're bothering the people next door. Can't you see your bed is next to the divider?" she said to my father sternly.

"What are you doing here?" she continued, addressing me. "If your father keeps behaving like this, we're going to have to move him to another room. We don't want the neighbors to complain."

I couldn't believe my ears. I began to hate that woman with a rage I'd never felt before.

"He needs pain killers," I told her, trying to control myself.

"We're giving him heavy doses of Klosidol. Other people who are worse off get by with less."

"But he needs something stronger. Each patient is different. I don't know . . . maybe some morphine?"

"You mean well," the woman said. "But you know nothing. You're asking me to cut your father's life short."

"I want to save him," I said, disconcerted. "Pain can kill, too; he could have a heart attack."

"Come to my office and we'll talk," she said.

I followed her with a feeling of repugnant happiness, because the excuse of saving my father from pain allowed me to walk guiltlessly out of that room where his whimpering sucked up all the oxygen.

"Don't go away. Get me out of here," he sighed again, painfully.

I followed the manager, who walked with small, genteel steps, always smiling, while she gave very precise orders to the house-keepers or nurses she encountered along the way. A starched shirt, buttoned to the neck, covered her heavy breasts, but her skirt was surprisingly short and tight: the hem almost dug into her fat, white, dimpled thighs, covered with thick blonde fuzz.

We went into the office, and she closed the door. Her office was just like her: all plastic and metallic sheen, proper and repugnant.

"Your papa behaves like a spoiled child," she said to me. "Don't be afraid—he's not going to die. Like so many people, you think pain kills, but you're wrong."

"Much younger people die of torture," I argued, uneasily.

"You said it, younger people. Old folks are different. You have to get to know them. They'll slip through your fingers from a bad head cold, and yet they can withstand amazing things. What kills them is some painful shock—sudden, acute. In your father's case, that danger is under control. Dull, constant pain, like he's feeling now, isn't harmful."

"I insist that you give him a stronger pain killer."

"You don't insist on anything around here. An opiate would be a stronger pain killer. Nothing better has ever been invented. Some morphine derivative: your suggestion isn't all that ridiculous. But, of course, there are side effects."

"What are you worried about? That a dying old man will become addicted?"

"I'm worried about the cost. Addiction is hard to sustain at any age, but that's nothing. I'm talking about death."

"Are you trying to frighten me by talking about my father's death? A man his age?"

95

"Why do you insist on connecting age with death? Just look at the statistics. In today's world, a newborn baby is more likely to die than an old man."

"It doesn't matter if we have to pay extra. If you don't have any morphine, I'll get some for you; I'll bring it, I'll inject it into him—it'll all be my responsibility."

"I'm the one responsible here. You can't free me from that. I don't know how much your father's life means to you, but it means a lot to me because my job is at stake."

She looked at me from behind her fake tortoiseshell glasses and smiled again, seemingly embarrassed at having gone too far, as if mentioning the worst possible punishment in this world—not death, but losing one's job—could be dangerous, or bring bad luck, or could magically attract the thing named. She tried again, using a different strategy.

"My personal opinion is that your father's life matters a great deal to you. It's not common to find children like you and your sister."

"Then you won't give him anything stronger?"

"Children disappear quickly. At first they start skipping their Sunday visits."

"You won't give him morphine?"

"I don't have that authority; I'm not a doctor. I can't prescribe. I don't decide what to give to patients. Don't worry. Try to see it our way: we want your father to get well and to live with us happy and contented for many years."

"Which doctor do I need to talk to?"

"It's not in our interest for the old folks to die. In the children's interest, yes, sometimes. This isn't an opinion, it's a fact. Don't take it personally."

She never stopped smiling.

Hatred grew within me until it flowed from my eyes, from my mouth. I don't recall ever having hated like that. In a strange way, the hatred concentrated in my sex, becoming desire. I wanted to rip off her plastic shell, squeeze her tits until they hurt, rape her painfully. I had never before felt such an urge to force my way into the body of such an intensely repulsive woman.

"Hit the floor!" shouted a sharp, hoarse voice. "Both of you! Now!"

It wasn't the first time we had heard that order. The manager and I threw ourselves on the floor without a moment's hesitation. I noticed that she managed to fall on top of a poorly concealed buzzer in the wooden floor. There were three attackers. Their faces were hidden behind ski masks—I thought, absurdly, that they must have been very hot out on the street—and they wore several layers of clothing, piled on top of each other so chaotically that they looked like madmen, vandals, rather than professional thieves. The one who gave the orders looked like a woman, although it was hard to tell.

Just as she fell, the manager took off a ring, rolling it into a corner. I would have sworn a moment earlier that it was just a piece of glass. All the hatred I had felt toward her began to turn into admiration and solidarity. My guts roiled, and terror crept up into my mouth, leaving a trail of fire in my throat. I listened to the sounds and voices without daring to raise my eyes from the floor.

"The keys to the pharmacy. Now."

They knew there was no money in a Home. They wanted access to drugs.

"In the desk drawer. To the right. Under a pile of envelopes," the manager said in a calm, even voice.

I felt oddly protected by her strength. One of the attackers opened the drawer.

With my face against the floor, I couldn't tell exactly when the guards arrived. It happened incredibly fast. As if in a dream, I saw the bodies react to the impact. The gunfire reverberated in my ears. I smelled a strange stench: blood and sulfur. Lying on the floor, motionless, trembling, I couldn't tell whether any of the shots had hit me. The assailants had assumed that the only guards were the ones at the entrance. They'd assumed wrong.

I heard the other security people running downstairs. I couldn't tell how much time had passed when I felt the manager's foot, wearing a shoe with a thick, high heel, pushing against my shoulder, trying to turn me over. It smelled like fresh earth. Only then did I manage to crawl to my knees. Each time I moved my head, a dark cloud blurred my vision. For the moment, my legs couldn't support me. No one asked if I was all right.

The manager was looking for something in the drawer. She took out a pistol that was rather small in relation to the diameter of the barrel. She approached each of the three bodies lying on the floor. I heard groans, but I couldn't tell where they were coming from, who was alive and who was dead. I was making uncontrollable noises myself. Without stopping to see if they were moving, she finished them off with an impeccable shot to the back of the neck.

"The police don't do anything with these guys. When they go to prison, they're in and out," she remarked. "Take them outside and have the girls come in and clean up."

Suddenly, she fixed her gaze on me, as if trying to remember what I was doing there.

"Was there anything else you wanted to tell me?"

At that moment, I was dragging myself over to one of the bodies, senselessly, without any conscious intention, like a reflex action.

"Were they looking for antipsychotic medication?" one of the guards asked.

"No, these guys are infected. They wanted expensive prescription drugs. I've told the staff a thousand times that it's dangerous to keep them in here."

Just then she discovered me, crawling toward one of the corpses.

"Where are you going? Don't go near them. And don't lift up their hoods—it's disgusting."

I managed to get out; I still don't know how. By some miracle, the inside of the Home was camera-free, but there were already a few amateur and professional photographers with their video equipment out on the sidewalk, taping the staff of the Home as they dragged the bloody bodies into the street and went back inside again to call the police. The guards overacted for the cameras with a sort of stoic indifference.

The taxi was waiting faithfully for me at the door. The driver had seen the attackers enter, but taxi drivers have complete confidence in their armored vehicles and in the service they render to everyone, without discriminating. Anyone who was able to get out of the Home alive would need a reliable vehicle. I opened the back door. As the car had new upholstery, I was circumspect enough to vomit on the street before I climbed in.

I looked at what I had vomited, and I vomited again.

18

I had an argument with my sister. I had asked her to help me get Papa out of the Home. I never imagined she'd agree right away, but neither was I prepared for such resistance.

"Papa's fat," Cora said. "He's a heavy man! He can't walk."

It was obvious we couldn't do it alone. I had already foreseen that. It wasn't enough just to bribe the guards—assuming that was possible—or to have a few nurses on our side. We would need help from both inside and outside. A team. And a large vehicle at the door, an ambulance or a station wagon. And then, where would we take him? Maybe it was time for me to make up with Margot: even if it's true I don't care much about her, I have no reason to remain distant. Now that I had no need to force myself on her body, we could be good friends. Margot would be thrilled to help me; she'd be painting the scenario in a romantic, adventurous light in order to compensate for my feelings of sordid sadness.

My sister, on the other hand, insisted on returning me to a reality that interested me very little.

"Getting him out is easy, trivial," Cora said.

That wasn't true, either: she hadn't seen the determination with which the manager had grasped the pistol.

"I've thought of a thousand ways to move him. But then, what'll you do with him?" my sister continued. "How do you plan to give him the care he needs? I can't even manage to turn him in bed by myself."

She was right. The IV, the medicines. I had some solutions, but not all. His secret physician had agreed, reluctantly and fearfully, to handle the case. But I didn't trust him: he could dump us at a moment's notice, even report us. Suddenly I understood that I had expected and even hoped for Cora's resistance. I needed an excuse to avoid carrying out a nonexistent plan, so I could blame others for my usual cowardice, my inability to act.

I usually get together with Romaris back at the apartment building. Talking is good for both of us. He needs to get used to his new, single existence, and I can't talk to just anyone about my father's situation, circumstances that so many people shrug off with indifference or with thankfulness. It's a show of friendship I didn't expect. (Could he be falling in love with me? Why can't I trust his friendship? Is it possible I consider myself so attractive, so desirable, to any man?) Alberto offered me his apartment for whatever purpose necessary. I didn't thank him for it. His offer to help obliged me to admit that my plans were better left theoretical.

I've acquired more clients for the famous gala, which is being talked about even outside film circles: the press, adequately fed, is beginning to spread fantastic rumors. Goransky recommended me to his friends, not just as a makeup artist but also someone who can be trusted. One of them, asking for extreme discretion, called me to work on his father. The guy was too old to try to disguise with makeup. In these cases, the best thing to do is accentuate the ravages of time to a ridiculous extreme so that it's impossible to detect where the reality of his old age ends and where artifice begins.

In this case, I had a good excuse. Eskimos believe in the existence of Tornraks, frightening spirits that only the great shamans can control. These Tornraks can assume any form, from the most natural—an iceberg, a seal—to the most horrific. The old man had investigated the subject at least as thoroughly as I had, and had very prudently requested that my makeup convert him into an Eskimo mummy, a cadaver preserved in ice, animated by an evil spirit. It seemed sensible and feasible to me. In a few hours, I created a serviceable mockup of what the finished job would look like. Underneath that simulated monstrosity, it would be impossible to tell how old he really was. The man seemed quite satisfied.

As I worked, I led the conversation toward the only topic that bursts from my brain these days. The old man explained all the measures he had taken to avoid being locked up in a Home. He trusted his lawyers more than his children, but he was intelligent enough to realize that without being in his heirs' good graces, the whole thing could fall through.

I love and miss my kids; I'd like to have them close by, but sometimes I feel relieved knowing that the burden of caring for my old, deteriorated body won't fall on them.

"Parents are parents, and children are children," the old man said.

And even though the statement made no sense from a semantic standpoint, it was the most concise, accurate way of explaining that parents love their children more than children love their parents, simply because they're the ones responsible for the children's existence and, for a long time afterward, their survival.

"And what if it all falls through?" I asked him.

"It depends. I might get used to living in a Home. We old folks love life, much more than adolescents do. But I'm prepared to change my mind."

He showed me the cyanide capsule hidden in the cavity of a molar. We know that not everyone is capable of using it, and no one can tell, until the final moment, if he dares take that bite. But feeling it there, being able to touch it with his tongue, must be a great comfort to him.

When we had finished, he offered me a nice sum to go to the gala and look after his disguise. I told him I'd certainly be there because several of my clients would attend. People feel more secure when they see me somewhere in the room, with all my working equipment. Parties last for hours. Perspiration, food, activity—they all take their toll. That upkeep business is the only part of my job that I hate—I don't like parties—as well as the most lucrative. I don't do it just for the money, though. Like any artist, I want my work to look perfect in the eyes of the public.

When I got home, there was a message from Margot. Her voice sounded friendly, even playful; it was her way of telling me she was sorry, and it touched me. Margot doesn't have a sense of humor, but she knows me. A sentimental phrase, a tearful tone of voice, would only have annoyed me, and I recognized how much effort she must have exerted to overcome her natural tendency to tragedy and record a friendly joke for me. I'll return her call.

I don't know why, but I've never expected to hear your voice on the answering machine. I don't know what I'd do about it, either. Keep it, I suppose, so I could listen to you whenever I felt like it. Never, in all those years, did you leave me a message: you never gave me that sign of confidence. You took every precaution. What could have happened to my unknown friend, that husband of yours whom you protected so? The last time we saw each other, you seemed so worried about him that it made me think of the children you never had. You told me his reaction to the separation was as painful as you'd feared. He was drinking a lot. Although I should have thought about the man you loved and not about my secret companion-in-misery, I still envied your husband, and I felt the pangs of jealousy in my chest, that sudden contraction of the coronary arteries that leaves you weak and breathless at first and gradually spreads, feeding your hatred with an immeasurable surge of blood, first a torrent, then a waterfall, rapids thundering in the arteries of your brain with a frenzy like howling wind; a real sound, perfectly audible. You seemed worried about him, not about me, and you were right, as usual: you can see I'm all right; you can see I'm still living, I'm managing; I can think about other things.

Other things. Papa's desperate words. Get me out of here. My father's voice, blending with my own childhood voice. But I was outside then, not inside. Because when my mother found it necessary to teach me a lesson, she would leave me, close the door and lock me out of the house. I was four, five, maybe six years old, and I curled up like a ball of yarn outside the threshold. I cried, banged on the door, pleaded: get me out of here, I cried, get me out of this loneliness, this cold, this abandonment, this terror. Get me out of here. After I reached a certain age, the punishment was no longer effective because I had acquired enough experience to realize that sooner or later, Papa would open the door for me, and besides, I'd learned to ask the neighbors for help. On the other hand, perhaps with the idea that a young girl always is in greater danger out in the street, Cora's punishment was for Mama to lock her up on the balcony.

And Mama? Only as adolescents did we begin to realize that Papa imposed the punishments and Mama carried them out. Papa always appeared to be saving us from a situation that he had thought up himself. Being forced to punish us was Mama's punishment. Papa's influence on her was enormous. Mama believed that if she didn't obey his orders regarding our upbringing, she would be responsible for all the terrible events that would destroy our lives. We'd end up in jail, we'd be injured or mutilated, we'd become permanent invalids, we'd die if she didn't learn how to control us, limit us, dominate us with a system of penalties that he invented for us. As a kid, I was afraid of dogs, and Cora was scared of bugs. Papa used his knowledge of our fears to invent punishments. It was a question of strengthening our characters. Later, Mama had to carry out the punishments. And he would save us from them.

Mama hardly ever spoke, laughed, or kissed us. My father had convinced her that she was too stupid to decide anything for herself. For a long time, he also had convinced us of the same thing. Like a blacksmith who shapes his work, he constantly hammered us with Mama's stupidity, pointing out her ignorance, her mistakes, her timidity, exhibiting her before others as well as in private. Papa had many friends: he was a jovial, friendly, amusing man, a prankster. But very few of them ever came to visit; very few were friends of both of them. Cora and I and Mama herself believed what Papa told us: that his friends had no interest in visiting a woman with a harsh disposition, always silent and bad-tempered. Later we understood how uncomfortable it was for people to tolerate the way Papa interrupted all Mama's attempts to enter the conversation, publicly calling attention to her mistakes.

When I grew older, I had the feeling that the only method Mama had discovered, in her enormous weakness, to confront my father was to become a kind of dead weight, a ballast he had to drag through life. Her lack of vitality, her bitterness, her indifference, served as a constant counterpoise to her husband's excesses. If he yanked the tablecloth off, upsetting the table, food, glasses, plates, bottles and all, she would simply pick everything up with no reaction, no comment, like a robot whose mechanism is automatically set in motion each time certain actions are taken.

You often pointed out that I never spoke of my mother. Motivated by your interest, I tried to give shape to a portrait that slipped through the cracks of my imagination. If my mother were dead, I could sit down with my sister and, between the two of us, we could try to reconstruct her. But she's alive; she's gradually metamorphosed, and now it's very hard for us to untangle her true personality from the undergrowth of confusion and delirium that blurs our memory.

19

Only a few times in my life have I seen my mother in the strange state of excitement in which I found her today. She seemed oddly happy. Her cheeks were flushed, and she had a confused, but intense, look in her eyes. Ever since she entered the Home, her behavior has appeared dominated by the drugs they tried out on her. Sometimes, like the last time I visited, we would find her totally devoid of emotion, indifferent to our presence, transformed into a piece of flesh that didn't care about anything, as if certain aspects of her normal personality had been exaggerated. And yet, when her emotions returned, as they had now, they were violent, massive, uncontrollable.

Mama took Cora and me by the hand. She said she wanted to tell us a secret and led us to the room she shared with another woman who was almost as absent as she was. She sat us down on her bed and told us, interrupting herself every so often with impertinent giggles, that she was in love. That she had become engaged to the boy who repaired the air conditioning. That he was young, but it didn't matter. That they were planning to have lots of children. That her only problem at the Home was a lesbian nurse who sexually harassed her. She looked at me, saucily sticking out the tip of her tongue, poking the withered, pale point of it between her sunken, cracked lips, deformed by a smoker's vertical wrinkles. She made Cora lean over so she could speak to her privately.

While on vacation as a child, Cora had had a bicycle accident, badly scraping her forehead and cheeks. Now, as Mama whispered in her ear, Cora's old facial scars began to turn red, as they always did when something made her blush. I tugged her away in order to save her.

"Let's go. We have to visit Papa."

Mama pouted. "My papa is sick," she told us, sniffling. "I'm afraid; he's going to die."

We walked through the corridors of the Home, so shiplike, toward the Intermediate Care unit. At times I had the sensation that the floor was moving, and I grabbed the handrail. Mama was following us. It was hard to shake her off. She didn't look unhappy. Each time we ran into a nurse, or one of the old folks, or someone from the cleaning crew, Mama celebrated the occasion with winks and funny faces. They all seemed used to it, and some of them replied by throwing her a kiss or nodding. Cora and I didn't even need to look at each other to understand that we were thinking the same thing: Mama might possibly be happier here in the Home than she had ever been in her life.

In my father's room, the beds were occupied by two skeletal old ladies, connected to various machines and in an apparently vegetative state. Papa wasn't there. But we could hear him grumbling.

Guided by the noise, I entered the room across the hall; the closed door muffled the sound of gentle, rhythmic moans. Isolated in his deafness and his pain, without his glasses, Papa couldn't see us if we didn't get too close to him. The manager was there, arguing with a doctor and two nurses. As soon as she spied me, she turned to me with a smile that contrasted with her accusatory words.

"Your father has an impossible personality," she said. "There's no reason for him to be having pain. Is there any reason, doctor?"

"None at all," said the doctor, without daring to look me in the eye.

"The neighbors complained again, and we had to change his room."

"Why don't you give him a sedative so he'll stop annoying people?" I asked hopefully.

"Ah, yes, I had forgotten. You're the one with the easy solutions. A nice dose of morphine and presto—no more problems."

Cora praised the new room, which to me looked exactly like the previous one. In the manager's presence, my sister took on a humble, understanding attitude, trying to agree with the woman's opinions, looking for arguments to support her.

"My papa's gotten old very suddenly," Mama said, approaching the bed. "Papito, darling Papito, I miss you so much," and she began to stroke his forehead with mechanical movements, like an obligation, but without affection.

"We'll have to insert a port at shoulder level in order to give him the IV, so we won't have to find a new vein each time. So he'll suffer less," the doctor said.

"Why don't you knock him out?"

"Because the anesthesia will be bad for him. There are side effects. If you father weren't so stubborn, if he'd drink liquid, we wouldn't have to hydrate him intravenously," the manager said.

"Papa's always been stubborn, you know that. He's always done whatever he felt like doing; the lady is right. It's as if she's known him all his life!" Cora said.

"Let's see if you two can persuade him to eat, so we won't have to insert a nasogastric tube," the doctor said, and for one moment I thought I saw a glimmer of pity cross his face.

"Leave me alone with him," I asked.

"We're going to put in the port. Then we'll leave him to you."

Papa was still incredibly strong, and the doctor knew it, because he asked for assistance. Two male nurses and the manager leaned over him, holding him down. Tying him to the bed wasn't enough. They tried to make us leave.

"Let me explain what you're going to do to him," I begged. "That's all."

"We'll explain it to him; don't worry," the doctor said. "Señor Kollody, we're looking for a good vein in your shoulder, understand?"

But without his hearing aid, my father couldn't hear him, and he didn't have the slightest idea what was happening to him. The four people who were struggling over him could hardly contain him in the bed.

"You have to shout into his ear! Can't you see he doesn't understand anything?"

"Get that man out of here," the doctor said.

And his three assistants let go of my father for a moment in order to attend to me. I showed my good will by leaving the room without their having to use force. Papa had recognized me and was following me with his cloudy, blinded eyes as he began howling once more.

Cora had left for Mama's room. I stayed in the corridor, listening to the uproar of my guts, which were rebelling as if each of my father's cries was a shot in my intestines.

"Murderers! Son!" Papa shouted. "Ernie! Save me! Help! Police! Murderers! Let my son in here!"

Afterward, I kept hearing inarticulate cries, wordless now, that rose from my gut, hitting me in the chest near my breastbone. What could that doctor be thinking as he worked on him? Sex and torture, inducing pleasure or pain: it's impossible to be closer to another person's body.

When everyone else had left, I went back into the room.

I wanted to touch him, but I didn't know where. His naked flesh peeked out here and there among the tubes and machinery.

"I'm going to get you out of here, Papito," I whispered in his ear. "I'm going to save you."

"I want to die in peace, Ernie," Papa told me. "I'm not going to be saved. I don't want to live, I don't want anything. I just want to die in peace. Promise me on your children's lives that you'll get me out of here so I can die in peace."

I promised.

20

In the northern provinces, in the old days, the dying used to rely on the Worrysnatcher. With a deft, twisting motion that compressed the cervical vertebrae, the Worrysnatcher would cut short the agony of hopeless patients.

They shoot horses, don't they? Our doctors oscillate between compassion and fear of malpractice suits. That's why there's been so much recent end-of-life legislation. But those laws don't affect the Homes, where each day brings the institution concrete financial benefits.

Now that I've seen them from an insider's perspective, I can understand Convalescent Home staff better. They're not pressured by the need to earn their salaries, nor have they received any special training. Training them would be insufficient: no matter how hardened they may seem, they wouldn't be able to resist the pleas of the dying if they weren't ideologically committed to the project. These are individuals chosen for their moral principles. People who, for religious reasons or personal beliefs, are opposed to mercy of any kind: because they have the peaceful, inner assurance that life matters more than anything else; or because they believe suffering in this world gives you credit toward the next one. You'll also find a few sons of bitches among them, but they're a minority.

Jotting down my ideas with pencil and paper, I made an inventory of possible ways to kill my father. I began with the most obvious ones: suffocating him with a pillow, hiring a hit man. I had had a long conversation with his secret physician about the swiftest, gentlest, and most effective ways to free him of pain. Papa has difficulty swallowing; this rules out oral medication. It would be very simple to inject whatever I wanted into the plastic tube that carries glucose and medication into his bloodstream, but there's a security guard permanently stationed in the room, and bribing one of them would be unthinkable. Not a single one would risk his job and possibly even his freedom just to facilitate my father's peaceful demise, not merely out of fear, but also out of conviction.

I threw away my list of ways to die and started another one: all the practical reasons why it was impossible for me to kill him or help him die at the Home, and when I had finished that list, I realized those reasons were false.

Papa hadn't asked me to kill him: get me out of here was what he had said; I want to die in peace. And that was I wanted, too, more than anything else in this world: to get him out of there and for him to know it. For him to live long enough to understand what I was doing for him. For him to be at my mercy, amazed and grateful. To have my father show me, for once in our lives, in words or at least with a look, a gesture, or through his very silence, even if it was just as he died quietly in my arms, to have him say in his own voice, or to make me feel in some way, what I had never heard him say: that he was proud of me.

I phoned Margot and we met for coffee. She appeared calm, in a good mood, ready to listen to me, and, as always, happy to share my misfortune. It did me good to see her again. Any sort of affection is a comfort these days. I'm going to ask her for help.

However, this time I decided not to speak to my sister. I'd never be able to convince her that we have to get Papa out of the Home, but I'm sure I can count on her once I get him out.

Romaris surprised me with an unexpected offer of help. His friend Sandy Bell, the transvestite who hosts one of the most publicized TV programs — that is, one of the most frequently watched shows — could lend us a hand in an emergency. Not everyone supports the Convalescent Home system; there are public and clandestine organizations that oppose them. Sandy Bell doesn't belong to any of these, but she's famous and wealthy enough to act on her own behalf in some cases.

I abandoned any illusion of intervening personally. I'm not cut out for violent exploits. Those eight thousand dollars my father lent me—or was it ten thousand?—and which I accepted in disgust at the time, would now be useful for paying off the people who would rescue him from his would-be saviors.

Today I went to an occupied zone.

Those of us who live in the no-man's-land that a good portion of the city has become are familiar with gated neighborhoods, where our rich friends, or our clients, or our employers live. Even just as guests, we enjoy the relative security of those placid, tree-lined streets. But I didn't know much about the occupied zones other than what I had read in the papers. People are aware that they exist; they talk about them, they read reports of crimes or police interventions, and they carefully avoid those streets that cross them. They even appear on maps, marked as if they were parks or plazas that one has to circle around.

Azcárate, the Charles Holstein hair colorist, took me there. There was a time when I told you quite a bit about him. It was when we were working together on some business venture or other: I did the makeup, and he was in charge of the models' hairstyles. Poor Azcárate nearly ruined two of the most beautiful girls trying to achieve a certain difficult color, a whim of the owner of Charles Holstein, Inc., who couldn't obtain that shade with his own line. One of the models ended up partially bald. With the other one, after several tries, they got the color they wanted, without losing the luster and volume of the hair, but the girl's face was so swollen and deformed by the chemicals that all my talent as a makeup artist couldn't hide it. It was in the course of that stupid disaster that we became good friends.

At Zum Zeppelin, where everyone bragged about whatever he could and where my friendship with Romaris would have provoked the dumbest jokes, Azcárate used to boast about his contacts with dangerous types. He spoke of raids on occupied zones; he bragged about certain great buys from wholesalers of more or less illegal substances that he sometimes offered us. To my surprise, his bravado contained a grain of truth.

Not every vehicle can enter an occupied zone. A cabdriver friend of Azcárate's, who looked like he knew his way around and wasn't afraid, took us there. Judging by the calm with which he drove, without speeding through the dangerous streets or worrying about stopping, I realized that there was some sort of identification on his car. I clutched my pistol in my pocket, trying to convince myself I'd be capable of using it.

The physical deterioration of the neighborhood was occasionally pathetic, but always frightening. Whenever slums aren't razed or changed by force, they undergo a positive transformation that gradually converts them into poor, but respectable, neighborhoods: the little cardboard shacks give way to little tin-roofed shacks, which in turn, slowly, wall by wall, are replaced by brick. In time they develop into humble, ill-painted houses, but always improving. In an occupied zone, the opposite takes place. Middle-class houses and other buildings, constructed of quality materials, experience a process of degradation that simple poverty can't explain. Only here, on their home turf, do the thugs have the possibility of expressing themselves perfectly, completely, without fear of any sort of repression. Their brains fried by drugs, or hatred, or boredom, and a frustration born of unemployment or God knows what, young and old alike destroy their own surroundings and systematically destroy themselves; and yet, instead of devouring one another and disappearing, they reproduce and grow like a dark, ragged-edged stain, one of the tumors invading the city like that blackish mass shining in the photograph of my father's intestine. The degradation is comparable in every way to the advancing cancer cells that transform different tissues, each one equipped to fulfill its own function—residences, shops, businesses, public or private agencies, plazas, streets—into a gray magma, broken down and filthy, where cables, garbage, weeds, walls, children, and animals swirl together in a confusion identical to itself, undifferentiated, useless.

Azcárate attempted to make jokes about the landscape. He didn't seem as relaxed as the driver. I, who knew a different city, felt terribly sad. Nonetheless, the man and woman with whom we had coffee and chatted were well dressed. The diction that emerged from behind their masks was like that of typical young college students. In order to find them, we had to go through a partially destroyed passageway. An alarm went off, and I had to turn my pistol over to a guard before entering a room that was as well—or as badly—furnished as my own apartment, with sufficient computer screens and the smell of real coffee. Azcárate hadn't lied to me: these weren't vandals but rather professional thieves who worked tidily and very precisely.

Money wasn't all there was to it. What I was about to pay was very little for such a risky enterprise. I should have given it more thought. The girl was interested in fine art and knew a lot about the subject, either because of its market value—they appeared to have contacts with collectors—or her own taste. Or maybe both. I offered them what little I had, childhood souvenirs, practically: an oil landscape by Russo and an Alonso portrait that I was given as a wedding present. The portrait was on a sheet of paper that had been crumpled up and thrown away by the artist. I always thought someone had taken the trouble to pick it up from the floor, iron it, and frame it in order to give it as a gift. But it was signed, and it interested them when I mentioned it. They were also interested in the fact that I was a makeup artist and promised me that someday we'd exchange roles: they would come around to hire me. It wasn't the type of job that exactly fascinated me, but I feigned interest.

Then it was true that Azcárate knew them well, and it was also true that they seemed to look down on him. I closed the deal with them as quickly as I could. We wanted to leave. The action would be carried out as soon as the paintings were handed over and appraised.

It wasn't the first time they had attacked a Home, but they would have preferred never having to do it again. Homes are dangerous. Many companies offer security guards for hire, but only chicken-shit outfits take advantage of that system. Big companies now have their own security departments that set up small, private armies. These armed forces aren't merely for defense. Furthermore, the security staff at the Homes is prepared to track down the old folks who escape on their own or with help: there aren't many of them, but they are ready for that eventuality. There, in that sort of secret cave, I heard the myth of the Old Runaways again. The guards at the Homes attack anyone who protects fugitives or who tries to prevent their return to the Home. Business is business.

21

He's asleep. It's possible he may sleep a few more hours. They handed him over to me with his hearing aid, his eyeglasses, his false teeth, and an adequate supply of morphine. The medication will help him slip peacefully over to the other side in the next few days. Or to rest in peace quickly if we're discovered. For the first time in a long while, I can hear his deep, even breathing, uninterrupted by moans. A man sleeping. Not suffering.

We're in Margot's apartment, in her daughter's bedroom. I wasn't at all surprised by her instant enthusiasm in collaborating. Part of her personality is the fact that Margot adores (until she gets fed up with it, and then she becomes dangerous) giving so much of herself that she becomes essential, a mother with eternally full breasts, ever ready to nourish the thirsty. I'm hoping this will be brief, that it will end before Margot gets tired of playing her role.

I brought over enough stuff from my place to spend a few days away. Some clothes, my toothbrush, the pistol. My faithful Sigma is a comfort to me: it's not likely to do me any other good. I take it out of my pocket, which is beginning to tear under its weight; I look at it, caress it, put it back again, wondering if I'll ever be brave enough—or frightened enough—to stick it against the roof of my mouth.

A while ago I made one of my habitual forays through the cable channels. But this time it wasn't a random excursion. When they turned my father over to me, they also told me at what time and on what channel they would show footage of the kidnapping. It was logical that they had clear pictures. Ever since the holdup at the Home in which I participated as a victim, ever since the guards threw those three corpses out on the street with a shot to the back of the head, there have been more video crews than usual stationed around the Home: blood attracts cameras like shit attracts flies. Better than honey.

The people I hired never described their plan of action to me. That's why I watched the program with interest, trying to reconstruct events from the visual image. The narrator, with fake innocence, spoke of a kidnapping. Since they couldn't bring the cameras inside the Home, and the start of the action was cleverly concealed, the footage began when everything was already almost over. Four people in helmets, masks, and exterminators' uniforms rolled my father out on his cot, looking as sound asleep as he is now. It was moving to imagine the sweat rolling uncontrollably down their faces, trapped behind their acrylic masks. I wondered exactly what had tipped off the video crews. Shouting, maybe, or unusual movement. The pictures were edited: the station had bought footage from two or three cameras.

It didn't seem easy to move a patient with such precision; besides the cot, they had to transport the monitor, the IV hookup, and other items that were impossible to identify. My father's body hadn't been disconnected from the machinery; he appeared to be surrounded by wires, and one close-up showed (puzzling to any other viewer, but not to me) the electrodes on his chest and the little tube of glucose that ended up in his shoulder. Very gently, they lifted him up onto the hydraulic ramp of the white van.

The kids had entered the home pretending to be exterminators. Had they held up the real exterminators' van? Or did they rig one up to look like it?

I thought they might have substituted the insecticide tanks with others filled with sleeping gas. Unfortunately, there were no inside shots of the Home. I imagined my friend, the manager, sprawled out on the floor with her fat, dimpled, hairy thighs more exposed than usual, sleeping with her mouth open while a thread of spittle dripped from her tiny teeth, forming a minuscule puddle.

The whole operation was carried out very calmly, until the two guards at the entrance intervened.

A closer shot of the guard's booth revealed how one of the guys, the bigger one, went over to the other one and grabbed him violently by the arm, as if trying to convince him to get out. The guy with glasses jockeyed his machine gun energetically, but wisely decided not to budge from the armored booth.

At this point, the picture jerked around uncontrollably: a clumsy amateur had tried to tape the shootout, moving the camera lens from side to side in order to follow the exchange of gunfire. It was very hard to figure out what was going on, in spite of the commentary that attempted to make up for the flaws in the picture. Most people like that sort of confusion, which confirms a certain popular notion of authenticity: there are even some expert filmmakers who deliberately take awkward shots to achieve that realistic effect. In the background, you could see a man with a camera talking to the van driver, no doubt telling him on what channel and at what time he'd be able to watch his own adventure.

Everything that had happened up till that moment seemed relatively foreseeable to me. All at once, a new horror began. Like tendrils of a grapevine that suddenly turn into writhing, supplicating animals, men and women who were too old, sick, or crazy to survive on the outside burst forth from the Home.

Isolated in a separate section of the Home, they were unaffected by the gas, by the shooting, or by fear. The sight of the staff and the other patients lying on the floor—that's what they looked like to me: sleeping or dead or frightened—hadn't affected them. All they saw were the open doors. Those repulsive, dying bodies thought only of escaping, of emerging toward freedom. Senile dementia, arteriosclerosis, Parkinson's disease, Alzheimer's. Names for the unknown, for what cannot be named. Those bodies that peeked out, pushing one another, falling, stepping on others who had fallen—the photographer, fascinated by the spectacle, had suddenly achieved a high degree of professional expertise—were endowed with faces I couldn't forget for a long time: perhaps worst of all were the vacant gazes, the crossed eyes, gleaming with madness, old faces with babies' grimaces, monstrous faces in the terror of delirium, arthritically deformed arms and legs attempting dance steps. My mother wasn't among them.

The old folks converged on the van with incredible speed,

considering their abilities, but infinitely slow for the assailants. One of the nurses had come out, too, and was already taking the situation in hand, placing herself at the head of the herd so she could direct the stampede by shouting orders. The woman seemed resolved not to let anyone escape. The van took off, advancing at a steady speed. For the moment, no one was following it. Toward the end, the narrator announced the next episode.

I liked the idea of sleeping gas and its possible side effects. If my fantasy turned out to be true, more than one elderly person would never wake up again; he would die sleeping, for his own good, hooked up to his nasogastric tube.

For the time being, I had become a fugitive. I wouldn't see my mother again, but she would continue to see me. It's a lucky person who can hallucinate another: he doesn't have to depend on anyone anymore.

As soon as it's light out, the secret physician will arrive. I've already ordered him a taxi. The man didn't want to get involved, but my description of the terminal symptoms convinced him. This is the end. If I just can spare my father the horrid treatment they dispensed at the Home, he won't survive more than two or three days, much less if we take away his IV. Death by dehydration is tough, the doctor explained to me. In a young, strong body, it's preceded by gangrene of the extremities, and it culminates in a scenario of slow asphyxiation. But with a person my father's age and in his condition, it'll all be over in a few hours. We can control the worst symptoms with morphine. We can elevate the dosage as much as necessary, without worrying about side effects.

It's possible that his final lapse of consciousness will be the one after this peaceful sleep, which I'm watching over tenderly. That will be goodbye.

At the last minute, I spoke with Cora. She replied indignantly. In no way would she participate in the plan. As though the wall of an ancient dam had split in two, her hatred of Papa, repressed for so many years, spilled out like a terrible ocean swell. She hasn't a single hope left; she feels nothing for herself; she won't accept a word of praise: she hates herself and everything else so much that revenge matters more to her than pride. Besides, it's very important to Cora to continue seeing Mama. I wonder, though, if she'll manage to convince the authorities at the Home that she had nothing to do with the kidnapping.

I won't be a fugitive for long. This isn't a matter for the official police force, traditionally understaffed, underpaid, and slow. The Home will send its small army of private security guards after us for a few days, and then they'll give up: they know all too well that the fate of fugitives is resolved swiftly. Even though they may know about or suspect my participation in this story, they have no power to teach the accomplices a lesson, nor do they need to do so: there are few cases like mine. Once in a while, an unusually strong or healthy old guy escapes by himself. But they don't get far. Their own relatives turn them in.

In a few days, this will all be over. In a few days, I'll be at Goran-sky's party, earning my living, touching up my clients' sweaty, and perhaps happy, painted faces.

Free at last of the image of my father drowning in pain, I'll be thinking of you again, as usual: once again, as usual, I'll imagine your face, contorted with pleasure; again, as usual, I'll feel your female form in the hollow of my hands in the fleeting visions of my insomnia. My father will have died a happier death than he deserves. And once more, as usual, my life will have no meaning.

22

By two in the morning, my father still hadn't awakened from his drugged sleep. I turned on the lamp on the nightstand. Margot's daughter was on vacation at the shore, so she'd installed us in the girl's bedroom. In my desperate anxiety, I couldn't stand being in the darkness beside my dying father. By the light of the lamp, the little girl's toys, broken and dirty, piled in untidy heaps, reminded me of certain circles of hell. But I managed to close my eyes anyway.

I fell asleep. I dreamed I was flying. With a single leap, I gained altitude and soared through the air, very high above the city. It was pleasant, and it filled me with immeasurable pride. In my dream, I realized that flying was very unusual. Only I, among all men, could fly, only I in the entire history of the human race. I advanced effortlessly, feeling the breeze against my face, floating with an ease I never had in water. Then, without any transition, we were in the country, and I had gathered together a group of acquaintances to watch me fly. I ran and leaped, trying to rise, but my leaps were just that: enormous leaps, twenty or thirty yards long, that lifted me quite a bit above the ground. No matter how hard I attempted to run full speed, to try every which way, it did me no good. In real life, these boundless leaps would have been extraordinary. In the dream, they were simply proof that I couldn't fly. The observers began to play poker.

A weak, frightening cry woke me in terror, my heart racing. I was lying beside my father in a narrow little bed that was stored beneath the other one. Papa had slid his head off the pillow toward me and had just let out a scream with his mouth right next to my ear. If my childhood memories didn't deceive me, it wasn't the first time he'd awakened me like that. I jumped up in bed with a start.

My father wasn't strong enough to lift his head, but his lips seemed to form a semi-smile.

"I'm thirsty," he said weakly. "I want some nice, cold club soda."

At the Home, they had told me the IV was necessary to hydrate him because my father wouldn't take any liquid by mouth. I ran to the refrigerator. There was no club soda, but I found an open can of cola.

I started feeding him the liquid by the teaspoonful. His stomach hadn't functioned normally for too long. I was afraid of making him vomit. Stretching his lips, Papa drank the cola, absorbing it, relishing it; he licked the spoon. His infantile pleasure touched me: his last pleasure, perhaps.

"It wasn't club soda, and it wasn't cold," he said, when half a glass was left. "Where are we? What a messy place!"

I explained that I'd managed to get him out of the Home, that I'd never again let them lock him up and torture him. I wasn't sure he'd understood me, but I didn't want to annoy him with the hearing aid.

"At that place, they really knew how to clean: it sparkled," my father said.

He looked scornfully around the room crammed with broken, dirty toys, and closed his eyes. He wasn't asleep, and he hadn't fainted, but he seemed powerless to continue speaking.

"Does it hurt you?" I asked with cruel egotism, happy to usurp the gigantic power of calming him, plucking him from his pit of pain. He didn't answer. He probably hadn't heard me.

"Do you want me to give you a shot?" I asked again, very loudly.

"I heard you. Don't shout; I'm not deaf. You just got me out of there, and already you want to finish me off?"

He was panting as he spoke, as if he needed air; he barely had enough muscular strength to articulate the words. Because of that, and because he didn't have his false teeth in, his diction was muffled.

"Didn't they explain to you that strong pain killers have side effects?" he continued.

With an enormous effort, he managed to turn over in the bed, clutching his sore belly, looking at the wall. It touched me: a strong, independent, authoritarian man subjected to the most abject humiliations—sickness and old age. He depended on me as a baby depends on its mother: but with less confidence. He resisted admitting it, fighting me, trying to affirm his independence with a word, the last word, the only thing he had left.

I had trouble falling asleep again. I went to the kitchen, took a glass of something that resembled milk but was much tastier, if one wanted to believe the ads. I turned on the radio, putting on earphones so I wouldn't wake anyone. The kidnapping of an old man from a Home isn't news for the radio, and it didn't surprise me that they hadn't mentioned it. These days, public attention is focused on the new economic package, and the radio devotes very little time to police reports, which show up so much better on TV, in living color. Without any deaths or money involved, the story would never find its way through the thicket of minutely documented crimes that invade TV screens every day. No one cares about this little story, except us. And the Home. But not for long.

The next morning, I found a phone center so I could call Cora, who was living with her friend. It's been a long time since anyone's used the telephones on the street, the remains of which still exist like ruins from another era. I was afraid she'd asked me if she could say goodbye to Papa. They might be following her.

"You're crazy," she told me for the thousandth time. "You think you're so good, a real saint. It's obvious you haven't lived with Papa for a long time."

"Do you want me to tell him anything for you?"

"Didn't you want to be a screenwriter? Tell him whatever comes to mind. Invent something."

"Did you see Mama?"

"They won't let me in."

"Cora, take care of yourself. In a few days, everything will be over, and we can talk calmly."

But nothing could be heard at the other end except her irregular breathing.

"I love you very much," I told her, and suddenly my voice took on a strange sincerity that startled me: it sounded like a goodbye.

Cora began to cry, and that relieved me.

Papa's doctor was coming out of Margot's building. He was very pale, and the wrinkles on his face looked like plowed furrows. He walked with difficulty. In an involuntary gesture, I grabbed him forcefully by the arm.

"Has he gone into a coma?" I asked.

He detached himself from me, ill-naturedly.

"He's eating breakfast," he replied.

I wouldn't have called it breakfast, but it was true that Papa was nourishing himself, propped half-up in the little bed, supported by pillows. Margot was spooning something soft and white into his mouth that I soon identified as bread dipped in milk.

"Bread? Are you giving him bread?" I asked, alarmed. "What did the doctor say?"

Papa wiped his barely stained mouth and beard with a napkin. He smelled of cologne. He was wearing his dentures now and smiled at me gently, with that strangely youthful, absurdly white acrylic smile.

"He said I could have whatever I want."

"You too? Are you worried about what might harm him? He's dying, isn't he?" Margot said.

At that moment, as if to guide the movement with which Margot extended the spoon toward his mouth, Papa lifted one of his big hands, with long, yellowish fingers, overgrown nails, and deformed knuckles, and wrapped it around Margot's hand. She was a bit startled.

"I think you can hold the spoon by yourself now."

"I think so," Papa said, fixing his watery, but still blue, eyes on her. "But your hands are so soft. Thanks for everything."

"He's saying that because I'm helping him get better," Margot said, looking at me a little uncomfortably.

"No. I say it because they're soft. And because you like to hear it."

But eating had worn him out. He was perspiring from the effort. We left the room so that he could rest quietly.

"What a strange, twisted image you have of your dad. He's not what you think."

"Do you think he'll need the morphine?"

"Maybe later. Not right now. His incisions are almost healed; all I did was to change his dressing."

As soon as Margot left for work, as though instead of sleeping, he had been aware of all the sounds in the house, Papa called me over.

"Nice ass, but she's kind of old," he remarked, regarding me with a bemused expression. "Is there anything else to eat?"

23

It feels funny, but not unpleasant, to be a fugitive. A whiff of adventure that breaks the monotony. Now I understand better how you felt whenever we were together: that joy of controlled escape that infidelity must produce in women. And the terror, always afterward. At times you were terrified to go back out into the street, even though a taxi was waiting for you at the door of the building. All the passion and savage delight you invested in sex had vanished, and nothing was left in you but fear. The moment of departure was the worst; you had fantasies of video cameras, as though your appearance were as compelling as an accident or a crime, as though you had my image stamped on your face, your clothing, your walk. To you, it *was* a crime, and at those times you acted ridiculously; you invented convoluted stories to explain your presence there to some imaginary acquaintance who might recognize you emerging from my house, as though each of your gestures, every one of your steps, was clearly marked with guilt and needed to be justified. You weren't afraid when you arrived, though, when you had newly escaped with a slightly giddy sensation of happiness and freedom, but rather at the precise moment when you started to feel like a prisoner again, about to return to your cell.

Now I'm the fugitive. Or maybe the prisoner. I didn't figure on the security guards reaching Margot's place so quickly. They weren't searching for me randomly: they were investigating my life. Romaris called to warn us; the guards had been to my apartment building, interrogating and terrorizing the neighbors. They had very likely already spoken to my sister. It wouldn't be too hard for them to find out Margot's address.

I myself had told Cora it wasn't necessary to keep it quiet for more than seventy-two hours. I calculated—a generous calculation—that this would be enough time for the guards to discover my father's body and certify his death to the authorities at the Home, who would in turn inform the operatives. They were authorized to use whatever force necessary in order to recover their prize pupil, but once he was dead, once the deal was lost, any violence against me would be pointless. The conflict would be reduced to a business negotiation, and in that territory revenge doesn't factor in, especially if the revenge costs money. Besides, I could defend myself physically and legally: attacking me after my father's death would have led to the risk of added losses with no prospect of gain. Everything was perfectly calculated.

The only hitch was that more than three days had gone by, and my father was still alive.

"You brought me here; you'll have to get me out," he told me, devouring a salami and cheese sandwich.

Margot looked at him, enraptured, believing that her ministrations and tenderness had snatched him from death.

I suddenly remembered the manager, her bovine teeth, her imitation tortoiseshell smile, the cruel intelligence behind that robotic politeness. I couldn't figure out what to do with my hatred. Toward her? Toward my father?

"Would you rather have stayed there? Did you like being with the manager, that stupid cow?"

"An intelligent, determined woman, with authority. Whatever she said got done. I admire people like that."

"You would have rather stayed there, with that piece of shit!" I shouted like a madman.

"Son, don't shout at me, I need you badly. Give me your hand, Ernie—can't you see I'm dying?" my father said.

And I wanted it to be true, but he was squeezing my fingers too hard.

"Why don't you two go stay at the downstairs neighbor's?" Margot suggested, avoiding the mention of Alberto's name.

"The guards have already been there."

"Exactly so. I don't think they'll be back. How could they possibly believe that Gregorio is already well enough to be transported so easily from one place to another?"

I regarded Papa enviously, suspiciously; I regarded him as I always did. A long, thick, impeccably white beard made him look Biblical, strong, even attractive. He had recovered his rosy, smooth, fat man's complexion. I waited for Margot to go into the kitchen for club soda. For the time being, as long as we needed her, it suited my purposes to keep her in a state of rapture. Her suggestion wasn't bad: after all, Romaris had offered me his house. I didn't want to call him from Margot's phone; if they had been in the building, the phones might be tapped. I would have to get Papa out and risk phoning my neighbor from the taxi. The poor guy had every right to regret his overly generous offer.

"You really didn't eat a bite for two weeks?" I asked Papa, making sure Margot wasn't listening.

"Not a bite is just an expression," he replied, chuckling. "Do you remember that nurse, the brunette—the one with the hairy mole? The ugly ones are the best: they're so grateful. She gave me spoonfuls of milk, secretly. And something else."

"We're going to have to get out of here right away. Right now. Can you walk?" I had good reason to think everything was a lie.

"I'm so sorry I'm not dead, son. I'm not saying this for my own sake; I'm happy. But I'm a burden. It would've been so good for you to shed tears over my corpse. No, I still can't walk. Being in bed for so many days has turned my bones to mush."

"If I call an ambulance, a taxi, how can we arrange things so they don't take you back to the Home?"

"Ernesto. Everything can be arranged. Is it possible a son of mine doesn't have any money?"

"The eight thousand you lent me all went into hiring the people who got you out of the Home."

"I lent you ten thousand," my father clarified. "The first two thousand were for paying off the interest."

Then he looked at me, shaking his head with smiling, compassionate disdain.

"Ernie, Ernie. Always overpaying. If a man isn't married by forty, it's unlikely he'll get married, but someone who hasn't earned money by fifty won't ever make any, that's for sure. Call my usual cab driver and leave it to me."

Margot cried as she said goodbye to us, making Papa promise he'd stay in touch with her. Between the two of us, we helped him out, pretending to be three drunks holding each other up, like they do in war movies when they're rescuing wounded prisoners. Instead of trying to go unnoticed, we sang out loud and laughed outrageously. Papa had enough strength in his arms to help us drag him along practically in the air, because his legs wouldn't respond. His erect position caused him plenty of pain, but he refused to take a sedative: instead of exaggerating his pain, now he was trying to hide it. If he occasionally cried out, we covered the sound with our voices. I carried a backpack with the most essential items of clothing. I called Romaris from the taxi to ask him if we could go to his house but also in order to make sure there were no guards left in the building.

"I'm not sure," Romaris hesitated.

He suddenly sounded frightened, regretful. He was right. He also had a good idea. We agreed to meet at a certain corner. Directions would be passed from one taxi to another.

"You'll go to Sandy Bell's house. I've already spoken with her," he told us, lowering the armored car window slightly. "She's such a good friend and a great guy."

I was surprised that Romaris changed pronouns randomly when he spoke of that transgendered individual. I had always thought they had a definite gender identity among themselves.

"What a lovely boy your neighbor is," my father remarked with an ironic half smile that expressed all the prejudices of his generation and perhaps also of mine. "Where's he sending us?"

I told him about Sandy Bell, the television personality. I thought he wouldn't know him, but he was perfectly aware of what it was all about. Old people watch more TV than kids. When he heard we were going to a guarded neighborhood, he perked up.

"You didn't even ask me once about Mama," I reminded him spitefully while the cab driver took us to Sandy Bell's neighborhood. Romaris had given him the password for the entry guard.

"Your mother's dead."

"She's not dead! She's crazy."

"Crazy, dead, what's the difference? The person we knew isn't there any more."

"You mean she can't do you any good any more, but she needs us."

"Crazy, my dear boy, crazy. Are you worried she'll miss you? You think she knows if she's seen you or not? Why think such nonsense?"

"Mama isn't dead."

"Fine. And since that's the way it is, why don't you pass me one of those tomato and olive sandwiches your lady friend made for us?"

Sandy Bell had left instructions for them to let us in. Nothing seemed to attract the guards' attention; they must have been accustomed to having Sandy receive all sorts of visitors. Or maybe those instructions applied to all guests entering the neighborhood: courtesy, indifference. The place was gorgeous: one of those areas of Belgrano with little chalets protected by a chain link fence, with the usual security booths. I had never been back since they closed it off. Some of the chalets had been demolished to expand the gardens or turn them into parks. There weren't many residents compared with other areas of the city, but they had enough buying power to justify the importance of the shopping center.

Everything surrounding Sandy Bell was exaggeratedly feminine, with that air of caricature one associates with transvestites. She had built herself the witch's house from Hansel and Gretel, with walls that looked like chocolate bars. The decorations on the windows, on the capitals, blinds, and doors, resembled sweets, as though they were made of multicolored candies.

She (he?) was waiting for us at the door in a kind of Marilyn Monroe getup, lacking only the blonde wig and beauty mark: a flimsy negligee with more lace and tulle than necessary, the classic high-heeled slippers with slightly worn, slightly dirty, big pink bows.

The interior of the house was predictable: typically fussy, with the *horror vacui* that defines bad feminine taste, crammed full of cute little decorations, prints on the walls, lace pillowcases with flounces on the armchairs. Sandy Bell welcomed us with an even higher-pitched voice than the one she used on TV and ushered us into the guest bedroom, papered in tiny flowers, where Papa plopped into a pink and white bed, unwillingly inhaling the rosy fragrance that impregnated the air.

24

We don't see much of Sandy Bell. Every night she performs live at the TV station. During the day, she films outdoor shots and special blocking in addition to supervising the rest of the production. She pays close attention to her relationship with the press: interviews and photo ops are part of the job. She also chairs the SB Foundation, which helps those people who want a sex-change operation but lack the funds, or those who have gone through the surgical-hormonal change and need psychological help in order to adapt, or who require legal assistance so that society will accept them.

Quite intentionally, she never comments on any matter concerning the elderly disabled or Convalescent Homes. That places her above reproach and allows her to help certain people with problems, as her adopted son explained to us. He's a skinny, sullen adolescent who must find it tough to contend with such a dad, who adopted him when he was a newborn. The SB Foundation also offers legal counselors for same-sex couples or nontraditional singles wishing to adopt.

Sandy claims to be around forty, and she (he?) publicly boasts that she's never had surgery, except for removal of her facial hair. In interviews she maintains that her breasts grew naturally, thanks to macrobiotic food. She has a gorgeous face, exquisitely feminine, but her height, her enormous feet, her broad shoulders and narrow hips, give her away. She conceals them by wearing bold gowns that display her (his?) shapely legs and are open down to her cleavage.

At a luncheon, I tried to make a pleasant remark about her gender switch and used the word "transvestite." Sandy reacted as if she'd been horribly offended. Patient, but annoyed, she explained the difference between a transvestite and a transgendered person. She considers herself a woman, an authentic woman in a male body, not an effeminate man. However, Sandy's indignation doesn't coincide with his public flaunting of his genitals, which he insists are intact, existent, and masculine.

Sandy Bell's kid seems very bothered by our presence and tries to avoid us, making us feel just as uncomfortable. But where else could we go at the moment? Cora knows where we are, through Margot, although neither one of them has Sandy's address or phone number.

Whenever I want to make a telephone call, I call for a taxi and leave the neighborhood. Sandy asked us to take this precaution: journalists are always on the lookout for sensationalism, no matter what it takes, and they're not satisfied with the foreseeable, controlled, and carefully organized excitement she constantly offers them. I've already gone out several times to get in touch with Goransky and my other clients. I've carefully organized schedules for the day of the party. I'm planning to start early with the less important jobs and stay there all night in order to supervise and retouch my work as many times as necessary. I've got nothing to lose, but nothing to fear, either. I'll have protection at the party. Even if the security guards from the Home look for us there, in order to get in, they'll have to deal with Goransky's security team, another small, private army. Besides, I'm sure the search has already wound down: no one has any reason to think my father is still alive.

Since we've been here, the famous transvestite—or transgendered person—has received reporters, photographers, or video cameramen at her home a couple of times. On those occasions, she locked us up in her study on the second floor so that no one would see us. Papa can climb stairs with help now, leaning on me. He can also stand up by himself—if he's sitting in a tall chair with armrests—and even walk a little, dragging his feet, inside the house; he exercises as much as he can. With a mixture of pride and horror, I watch him improve every day.

"Like Bluebeard with his women," Sandy explained to us, winking coquettishly, "I let the photographers into all the rooms but one. A good public secret turns them on. If by chance someone manages to get in while you're there, you can hit him on the head with a stick: that's what Bluebeard would do!"

It's wise of her not to let the photographers into her study, which has a fine library, a blond wooden desk, a multimedia device with a giant screen, and a couch, but above all, a very subdued ambiance, with colors that harmonize without clashing and are altogether devoid of any shade of pink. The room differs dramatically from the rest of the house, especially from Sandy Bell's alleged bedroom, crammed with dolls and stuffed animals—cats, bears, and rabbits—where the hoariest, most ridiculous notion of the eternal feminine has been taken to the ultimate extreme. Sandy sleeps in her study.

Whenever we run into Sandy, my father fixes his gaze on him with greater curiosity than politeness allows. Once, when we were hiding in the study, I discovered him trying to open a locked box with a plastic card. I grabbed it from his hand: he's still weak enough to be controlled by force.

Gary, Sandy Bell's son, is one of those unreadable, indifferent boys who wander through shopping centers smoking a joint with a life-is-shit expression on their faces.

Recently I learned through the security people that a group of neighborhood kids, slightly older than Gary, had tortured a neighbor's dog by putting three screws in its head. A few days later, the dog still remained in a coma, and I couldn't tell if my feeling of nausea and horror was directed toward the torturers or the dog's owners, who were prolonging its agony with all the scientific means at their disposal, ignoring the mercy usually afforded to animals and making it suffer as if it were human. No one suspects Gary, and with good reason. It doesn't seem possible that the boy would be capable of emerging from the haze of ennui and contempt enveloping him—even if his eyes do look so penetrating sometimes—with enough energy to screw three bits of metal into a dog's hard skull.

But in spite of appearances, Gary has a passion. And if he keeps it a secret it's not only because it's a forbidden, unsavory, or provocative passion: what he wants to hide is the passion itself, that burning interest which might modify or destroy his image of perfect indifference.

134

Was that how it was with you? How did you hide me when you weren't with me? What words, what expressions, did you use with your friends without mentioning me? Sometimes I would take a taxi to a shopping center with you just to be able to watch you walk by yourself, to see how you walked away without me, to observe your gait, your disguise. I enjoyed playing with the illusion that your entire life beyond me served only to conceal me, to keep others from reading your desire. I liked to think that I, we, our passion, was so omnipresent in your mind that you had to fabricate a permanent indifference toward everything else in this world so you wouldn't betray yourself. Pure fantasy: you wouldn't have fallen in love with someone else if you had loved me as I imagined, as I loved you.

Even though you told me very little about him, I already knew everything. Was it really necessary to say anything more than his name? I didn't, and still don't, want to think about that story: about his too-familiar face, your regret, your curiosity, what I might have done or said to awaken it, the machinations you invented in order to meet my father, the methods he used in order to seduce you.

You were crying, and you didn't have a Kleenex, and I refused to give you one. I watched you cry as if I were behind a thick, foggy window. I couldn't stand up because my legs wouldn't support me, and I watched you cry with absolute coldness and detachment. With that calmness, that iciness, I was distinctly aware of not dragging myself along the floor, of not hugging your knees, begging, because I knew it was useless: for that reason alone. With that same calmness, that iciness, I wanted to tell you it didn't matter if I had to share you with anyone, in any way, that I was prepared to accept anything, any scrap, any speck, any broken, filthy, useless piece of your time that you were willing to give me.

But you couldn't do it; you wouldn't. You were horrified at what you'd done, remorseful. You were too concerned about my dignity, and you were right. I watched you cry, calmly, coldly, lucidly; I watched you wipe your nose on your sleeve, and I wouldn't give you a Kleenex because, at that moment, that was my only power, my only revenge.

25

It was always hard to conceal anything from my father, so curious, so eager to control even our dreams. It's impossible to hide a secret from someone who wants to know and who has no principles, no scruples, nothing to prevent him from turning you upside down and opening you up to inspect your crevices or your guts. It didn't surprise me, then, that in just a few days my father became such good friends with Gary, Sandy Bell's boy.

Gary was at the stage all adopted kids go through at some point: he was searching for his real mother. It wasn't too hard for Papa to get him to talk about the only idea buzzing around in that head which was empty of all other thoughts.

The boy helped him with his exercises, walking him from one end of the room to the other, leaning—with increasingly less support—on his shoulder. One afternoon I caught them looking at some of Gary's most secret treasures. They were photographs. I thought I spied one of a pregnant woman before they realized I was there.

How could I warn Gary about the person in whom he had decided to confide? I myself felt like a fourteen- or fifteen-year-old boy, younger than my own children, a kid prepared to believe in any adult who paid enough attention to me but at the same time knowing, with the absolute, but unverifiable, certainty of dreams that I would be betrayed. Whenever I saw the old man patting the boy on the head or cuffing him lightly and companionably on the shoulder ("Champ," he called him), I felt pity. Or jealousy? Was my father finally capable, now, at the end of his life, of feeling and expressing emotions that had been denied him in his youth? Emotions that had never been destined for me or for Cora but which, nonetheless, were still possible for him to feel?

In the face of his unexpected recovery, I tried, for the first time in a long while, to form some kind of long-range plan: where to go, what to do, how to live from now on. We'd have to get out of the city. Goransky's party was the deadline I had imposed on myself for making certain decisions. My funds were drying up. Papa had gone back to his old tricks: he was behaving like an indigent old man and refused to contact his attorney.

Then, early one morning, the neighborhood sirens went off. Piercing, dramatic. Although I didn't know what it meant, I ran to awaken my father, who was sleeping without his hearing aid. Gary was already there, shaking him and helping him stand. For an old man, even one in full control of his body, getting up from a low bed is more than his strength permits.

"It's the security guards from the Home. Let's go," I told him calmly.

We would try to escape. What difference would it make if we didn't succeed? I had no compelling reason to preserve my own existence. What did I really want to do with my father? Keep hiding him? Or turn him in so that they'd take him back once and for all? I examined my conscience candidly, realizing how betrayed I felt because he hadn't died when it suited my purposes. The siren kept wailing.

Then we heard Sandy Bell's urgent, desperate, unrecognizable voice: a warm, serious, feminine, contralto voice instead of her usual high-pitched warble.

"They're raising the barbed wire fence!"

We ran to the secret hiding place, a basement whose existence I knew nothing about, reachable by lifting a trap door hidden in the parquet tile floor. Sandy made us enter single-file. He seemed crazed with fear. It was the first time the siren had gone off, the first time an invasion was more powerful than the security force protecting the neighborhood. The lights went out. In the darkness it was difficult to force my father, who was whimpering in pain, to enter.

As we stood elbow to elbow, surrounded by absolute blackness, I felt a strange sensation. Sandy Bell's body brushed mine, and I felt something more than I would have liked, a tingling in the groin that hadn't quite become—at least, not yet—desire. It was her scent. In her nightgown, still wrapped in the warmth of her bed, without the halo of French perfume that usually surrounded her, Sandy Bell gave off a warm, swampy smell, like overripe fruit. She smelled like a woman. Without thinking, I put my arm around her shoulders.

Gary lit a match. Sandy made him put it out immediately, just before the invaders entered the house. But we were all able to see her without her disguise: without the shoulder pads, she no longer had broad shoulders. Her bare feet were small and her hips shapely.

We stood there, motionless, in absolute silence, sensing the chaos that was going on above our heads. It wasn't the guards. Once more, we could hear the classic blows, gunfire, explosions. I don't know how much time went by. I think I may have slept intermittently. Later I learned that everything was over in less than half an hour.

Someone was raising the trap door.

"Those are our people. The security people." Sandy's voice, nestled against me, roused me from sleep.

"Congratulations on the great security service! How much do you charge?" Papa asked sarcastically, already upstairs. "Because if you're not too expensive, I'll recommend you."

When I emerged, I could better appreciate the irony of my father's remark. Sandy Bell's little candy cottage looked like a tornado had swept through it. Everything that could have been broken was broken. Everything that could have been knocked out of place, was. Part of the house had been destroyed by a modest explosion that had demolished half a wall without managing to destroy the columns or beams.

Sandy Bell was curled up in a corner, refusing to come out of the hiding place as long as people were still in the house. But when she learned that the security team wanted to ask us some questions, she asked me to hand her her clothes, and she emerged with enough energy to throw everyone out of there and fling herself down for a good cry amid a jumble of debris, broken glass, garbage, and papers.

Glassy-eyed and in a state of total agitation, Gary went over to her, stroking her head.

138

"I knew, Mama," he told her. "I've known for a long time."

A touching scene, but we had to go. From the security people's questions, we understood that they still didn't know if it had been a guerrilla attack, an act of revenge by drug dealers, a professional robbery disguised as an act of vandalism, the work of one of those religious groups that advocate violence, or a true assault by vandals, the kind no one claims responsibility for, no one can explain, one for which the lack of motive makes it impossible to find the perpetrators.

The attack had been swift, perfect, proving that a team of inside people had cooperated. In hours, perhaps minutes, the security company would begin its investigation. We had to go.

Goransky was the only one of my acquaintances who had enough money and power to help us get out of there. Would he be willing to do it? With my father barely learning on my shoulder, but walking on his own and fairly erect, I left, without much hope of finding an intact cell phone in the neighborhood.

"Poor Gary," I attempted ironically, "he had to lose his adopted father in order to find his real mother."

"Poor fool, you mean: believing that gentleman was his mother. Don't you know what they can achieve these days through surgery? Even with bones?"

At that point he noticed my perplexed expression, my naked face, and he realized that I, just as much as Gary, wished that Sandy had been born a woman.

"Not just with surgery: also with hormones, naturally," he added. "Plenty of hormones, in order to get results like that!"

And he laughed, my father did, as if he'd never stop. With an eternal belly laugh, he laughed at my insignificance, my innocence, my doubts, my skinny legs, my attempts to develop my muscles by riding my bike night and day. As usual, he laughed at me.

26

If you spell out the word "eternity" in blocks of ice, I will give you the whole world and a pair of skates. That was the Snow Queen's promise to her jubilant prisoners. The scene designers working on Goransky's party had managed to transform Retiro Station into a palace.

Just like the Snow Queen's palace: walls of compacted snow, the storm as orchestral background, doors and windows of piercing wind. Walls metamorphosed into false horizons to create an impression of infinity. And yet there was nothing monotonous about it, a blinding repetition of pure whiteness: the enormous reception hall was illuminated by the Aurora Borealis projected on the walls and ceiling, or perhaps on a warm cloud that formed up above, blazing in such a way that it was impossible to locate the artifice behind all that brilliant color.

For most people, Retiro Station was an ugly, run-down, dirty, dubious sort of place. For one brief spring it had been restored by the railroad company, but it soon was overtaken by sadness and poverty again. Nevertheless, for those who could detach themselves from this everyday, superficial appearance, the palace was already there, behind and beneath the rubbish, the people, the booths where *chorizo*, sandals, candy, lemons, garlic, and dreams were sold. Retiro Station was built and designed in the British style, with a high, vaulted ceiling supported by beams made in Liverpool, marble columns and floors, sculpted awnings, sunbeams that emphasized its height, and everything a cathedral might possess with the exception of altars. Goransky's architects knew how to envision and exploit potential.

When the guests arrived, they left their armored vehicles in the sham reindeer stables, precariously constructed in the parking lot. There they were greeted by dwarfs dressed up as Santa Claus's elves.

By renting the station for the party, interrupting the arrival and departure of trains, Goransky had caused a new kind of chaos in the city's transportation system. That chaos was part of its success. The spectacular effects created more publicity for the party, giving it top coverage in the media. Journalists criticized the immorality of certain practices that were detrimental to the common good, and the party became a topic of public conversation and comment throughout the country.

To avoid monotony, the immense hall had been divided into sections with varied décor, where different activities took place. There was a Bear Dance, with real bears, under the supervision of trainers who intermingled with the guests, disguised as bears: the costumed humans turned out to be more realistic, or maybe just more graceful, than the bears themselves.

There was a tea for Arctic foxes. And a cluster of Lapp huts, where exquisite dishes were served, not always in keeping with the central theme of the party as far as ingredients were concerned, but authentic in their presentation. The roofs of the huts sloped to the floor, and in the terribly hot interior, attractive, sweaty men, bare-chested and dressed in reindeer hide pants rolled up to their knees, served oysters shaped like snowflakes with white sauce and meringue, and extra-tender unborn veal steaks rotating over a fire, as if they were a single slab of flesh stuck to the enormous femur that served as the central skewer: a bear leg.

There was a frozen lake, broken into a thousand uneven pieces, where guests could skate without tripping because the "cracks" were painted on. In some places, a bevy of snowflakes fell on the tables or on the igloos. The snowflakes took on strange shapes as soon as they hit the ground: hedgehogs, spiders, little bears, unidentifiable shapes, all of them with lots of legs that made them creep up the walls, suddenly white, and fall again and again, like water from a fountain.

Among the guests, only the youngest could enter the igloos, by crawling through the entryway. Inside, they feasted on chunks of seal meat, delicately rotten, dripping fat over the central fire.

All the myths and realities associated with the Great Chill were represented simultaneously. All the tribes. Lapps, Eskimos, fantastic Ona and Patagonian Indians, denizens of Greenland, native Alaskans. All the animals of the North and South: anyone who scrutinized the seals carefully could see how the costumes replicated the differences between various species. There were walruses and manatees, sea lions and elephant seals, each with its appropriate fur, snout, and whiskers. There were monarch and emperor penguins, ska birds, terns, polar starlings. There were exquisite women whose features were accentuated by a skillful makeup artist, blending beauty and cruelty to represent the Snow Queen. There were thin men with fake bellies and stuffing in their cheeks dressed as Santa Claus.

I examined my professional colleagues' work with interest, and gradually I was filled with the pleasant reassurance that I was still the best, or at least one of the best. The usual experts had concealed their clients' faces beneath thick layers of putty to imitate caribou's or Arctic foxes' snouts, but they had all followed the dictates of popular convention about the North and South Poles. Only I—with the exception of my client who was dressed as a mummy—had studied Eskimo culture enough to create those haughty spirits of Good and Evil, the Tornraks. Goransky was pleased with my work; he felt splendid: the greatest, strongest, most terrible of Spirits, adorned in the red of fresh blood shimmering on the snow. His satisfaction, the self-confidence he derived from the makeup that concealed and showed him off at the same time, guaranteed me future jobs, the certainty that if his film were ever made, I'd be right there and not at the bottom of the credits.

I also experienced the wicked joy of seeing Goransky's new (and now former) screenwriter, my immediate replacement, that young, skinny, messy-haired girl I had spied him with in the study during one of his moments of cinematic inspiration. The woman was wandering around in a daze, wearing a cheap Eskimo costume that hung from her frame as though she were trying to escape it. Enclosed in Goransky's study with my father, I had heard the staff gossiping about how the girl had overreacted when she found herself so suddenly replaced. Nonetheless, she didn't want to miss the party: no one did. Even my father had insisted that I disguise him completely with makeup so he could attend the party safely, but I refused to take him along. It wasn't that I expected to run any risk; it was just that I was tired of him, and I wanted to enjoy myself and work in peace, without criticism, without witnesses. It was tough to convince him that he wasn't yet well enough to spend several hours at a party.

There were fire-eaters, politicians, acrobats, journalists, athletes, clowns, historians, political analysts, actors, belly dancers, and sociologists. The motley TV crowd had mostly chosen the sort of clever costume that emphasizes instead of concealing. From a distance, I spied Sandy Bell dancing, magnificent in her incarnation of a drag Snow Queen: man? woman? For some stupid, uncontrollable reason, my body (my mind?) keeps harping on a question that no longer matters today. I stayed away from her.

My clients kept me very busy, especially Soledad, Goransky's wife, disguised as a young Eskimo woman with violet eyes. She kept worrying that her real skin showed through the layers of makeup, as if her features were sharp enough to cut through the game of illusion. After several trips to the dressing room, I handed her a little magnifying mirror so she could monitor her appearance without driving me crazy. I hate mirrors, she told me, and I hate the magnifying ones even more. I ignored her.

The Eskimo mummy, on the other hand, that bright, endearing old man, navigated the party with the rare joy that only an absolute lack of hope can bring. His costume permitted him to walk around, relaxed, displaying the curve of his old back, emphasizing his limp, his slightly tottering gait, his reddened, cloudy eyes.

I had asked Goransky to invite my sister so I could talk to her in the crowd, surrounded by so many witnesses that no one would see us. I had been wandering around in the hubbub for over an hour, annoyed with myself at not having asked Cora to describe her costume in more detail. I myself was a huge seal, and my eyes, hindered by the small openings, squinted out, concealed, at neck level. It was like being inside a puppet, although the openings beneath the flippers allowed me to stick my arms out so that I could work comfortably. Only the party staff wore costumes that hid their features and physiques completely. I could have chosen to disguise myself as anything, but I felt more secure inside my puppet suit. Despite the fact that logic assured me I was safe, I thought I could detect costumed guards from the Home everywhere.

And your face, naturally. There, as in so many other places. Because I find it impossible to be in a place packed with people (a theater, a shopping center, a party), disguised or otherwise, without the desperate hope that I'll see you, even though I know you're not there. And I did see you: I recognized your fleeting profile, for example, which I know all too well, much better and more intimately than other angles of your face: so many hours of talking, lying next to each other, looking at each other sideways. I thought I felt your hair brush against me; suddenly, the contact of a hand on a face made my skin tingle, but when I tried to confirm with a direct gaze what had tantalized me from the dubious edge of my field of vision, you disappeared again, lost once more amid all the men, all the women.

I ran into Cora emerging from a Lapp hut, barely disguised, perfectly recognizable, searching for me inside every seal. We didn't embrace, but I took her hands and squeezed them tight. I felt the hardness of Mama's engagement ring, the solitaire that Cora wears now with the stone always turned around toward the palm of her hand so thieves won't be tempted. It hurt me a little, but it also made me feel good.

"Where's Papa?" she asked immediately, in a tone of voice that sounded more like fear than love. As if confirming my feeling, Cora stared at the people around me, wide-eyed.

They had interrogated her. She was afraid they were following her; she imagined they were wiretapping our phone conversations. She would never have dared come to the party if she hadn't been picked up by a chauffeured limousine and the little security squad provided by Goransky, who was strutting around acting like a big shot. My own composure calmed her down. She exaggerated the strength of the Home's private army. There weren't so many of them; they weren't so efficient; they couldn't wiretap all the phones on the planet.

Only Cora, of all the people in this world, could understand my uneasiness and despair, my doubts about my father and our future. Mama was fine. They had let Cora see her. Mama didn't recognize her, but she appeared to be serene and even happy, as we had seen her lately. For the moment, my plan was to get out of the city with Papa: Goransky had offered me his country house. Cora mentioned the community of Old Runaways again. If only I could believe that ancient myth: a marginal community of free, happy people, united in rebellion. For any respectable family, it was as effective a way to rid themselves of their old folks as a Convalescent Home. For the old folks, it meant something more than freedom. An illusion of independence and power, a sort of country of their own where they themselves ruled but where no one but they could attend to their needs: a mythical paradise where they were monarchs and slaves.

Cora had never had many opportunities for happiness in her life, not even fleeting pleasure. I myself had dismissed her for years. Now I was sure that I also needed and loved her. I invited her to join me in the bear dance, and we began swaying clumsily among people and animals.

As we danced, we noticed a collective movement toward one side of the hall. It was as if the entire party had begun to shift toward the staircase; those who couldn't get close turned in that direction. All the comments were tinged with scandal and admiration, and all were directed toward the same place. We tried to draw closer so we could find out what was going on.

Goransky was introducing a special guest, in a *mise-en-scène* of his own devising. The idea, the libretto of the presentation, the dialogues, everything seemed to be excellent, judging from the powerful effect it was creating throughout the hall. We managed to elbow our way to a table where other guests had had the same idea and were standing on top of the chairs.

27

The clatter of cutlery, the applause, music, footsteps, that intense rumble that can be heard only in seashells and at parties, was suddenly cut short. The silence became a solid mass weighing on the party, like an enormous iceberg threatening to flatten the tinsel decorations. There, atop the improvised staircase that all the guests had to climb in order to enter and be announced with a trumpet fanfare, next to Goransky, who grasped his arm for support, stood my father. *Sans* costume. *Sans* makeup. He advanced slowly, leaning on the cane, with his strong old man's gait, his long hair, and his pure white beard. Magnificent in his splendid senescence.

When my father suggested the idea to him, Goransky must have drooled with joy. In the days when we were working on the script together, he always tried to interrupt the story development in order to superimpose more or less incongruous scenes in which a certain visual effect would be sure to move, grab, or seize the attention of the audience, which, according to him, was distractible, liable to get lost in the labyrinths of their own minds. I don't want our audiences sitting in the movie theaters like so many people do at a concert, thinking about something else, he insisted: you've got to shake them up, not let them drift off; you've got to bring them back.

However, neither one of them had calculated the impact of their audacity. My father descended the flight of stairs amid a worrisome silence. As he started to walk through the hall, the guests moved aside, awkward and frightened, to make way for him. In the silence, the bands, which acoustical experts had carefully arranged to be heard separately in different areas of the party, divided by walls of noise, blended their voices in a sort of crazy chorus, only to fall suddenly silent.

Goransky realized how outrageous his proposal had been, and now he hurried down the stairs with the intention of taking my father's arm, herding a group of guests together, calling for champagne and celebration and cracking a few jokes that would make everyone forget the whole incident and return to the party in good spirits.

Papa, on the other hand, at the pinnacle of his triumph, didn't take notice of anything he hadn't foreseen, and he was smiling as much as the solemnity of his role would allow. He had spotted us and was coming over, opening a kind of wound in the compact mass of guests who moved aside at his approach. There were many old folks at the party, feigned or exaggerated in various ways, but no other genuine Elderly Person prepared to show his face in all its majesty. He was the Mask of Red Death, sowing terror, carrying pestilence, pain, and death to the unwitting guests of the Prince. Only his face didn't look like a mask (it was the only one that didn't), and no one would attempt to yank it off just to discover that underneath it was nothing but emptiness. He was Red Death itself, parading in all its splendor.

Suddenly a group of guests (seals, Eskimos, reindeer) bravely detached itself from the trembling mass and surrounded him. At Goransky's signal, the closest band began to play, and a couple of waiters dressed in whale suits came over with hors d'oeuvres and beverages. With a nearly audible collective sigh, the party resumed; the compact masses dissolved and scattered again throughout the hall. A gurgling murmur drowned out the music. A fat, cheerful Mrs. Santa Claus asked my father to dance. Without releasing the cane that supported him, Papa stepped onto the dance floor with a certain dignity that attracted glances.

"What do they have in common?" Cora asked me just then. "Look at the group over there with Papa. They all have something . . ."

Cora, always so absent-minded, so inattentive to the hallmarks of reality, noticed it before I did. They had something, indeed. Hard to define. A certain style, maybe. As if they had all ordered differ-ent costumes designed by the same tailor. It was obvious to me that their faces had all passed through the hands of the same makeup

147

artist. A family? A bunch of friends? Those weren't the answers my fear suggested.

I got close enough to see the broad smile on the woman dancing with my father. In the whirling of the waltz, she appeared to be pulling away—so slowly that it was hard to be sure—toward one of the exits, while several couples furtively followed, whirling along with them.

The broad smile: those even, unmistakable, old cow teeth. Her fat thighs, sheathed in billowy, red satin pants with fake white fur cuffs. I approached Papa, whispering in his ear.

"Let's go," I told him simply.

"He's my son," Papa introduced me. "A good boy. When he was little, he used to bite his toenails. Now he's a little jealous, but he'll get over it."

As usual, he was talking to me while addressing someone else.

"They're people from the Home," I whispered.

The woman, without dropping her smile, without interrupting the dance, had lifted her arms, tossing the loose, fur-trimmed, red sleeves backward. On her left arm, she wore something that looked like a wristwatch on a thick, platinum, leash-like chain. She initiated a maneuver with her right hand, as though she were winding the watch. Papa spotted it before I did: they were handcuffs. He escaped in time and tried to run away as fast as his old legs would carry him. The woman thrust one hand into a false pocket in Mrs. Claus's enormous belly, and, without pulling out the weapon, fired noiselessly, blindly, through her suit. A long-lashed lady bear that was standing behind my father fell, moaning, to the ground, clutching her chest. You couldn't see any blood; maybe the bulky costume had absorbed it. Those who were with her didn't even hear the shot. Someone shouted for a doctor. I imagined they had fired some kind of tranquilizer gun.

It all happened too quickly. I didn't know what I was doing. My father took a step sideways and grabbed my flipper, almost tripping me, but he achieved his goal: he thrust us both into the middle of a compact mass of dancers very close to the orchestra. Goransky's security people tried to intervene discreetly in order to avoid panic, while the guards from the Home surrounded Mrs. Claus. Panic had already set in, however, and was beginning to spread in concentric circles, like water into which a stone has fallen. Thanks to the fact that we were a few seconds ahead of the first wave, we managed to sneak into the stables.

Ignoring the commotion caused by the elves, we climbed into the first available vehicle (they all had their keys in the ignition; I chose the one closest to the exit), rolled up the armored windows, and slammed against the barricade. My seal tail was bulky, and the head of my costume bumped against the roof of the car. I hadn't driven in a long time. The car had an automatic transmission, but my foot stupidly searched for the clutch. I floored the gas pedal, but it didn't pick up right away. I couldn't see what was happening very clearly; the sensations were recorded in my brain, but I couldn't make sense of them. My father was silent; he had depleted all his energy to get to this point, and he collapsed on the seat, exhausted, lacking even the strength to fasten his seat belt. His face was ashen. Before breaking through the barrier, I felt—and disregarded—a crunch, the left wheel running over something soft, noisy, and unidentifiable.

I eased up on the gas pedal as soon as we were outside. It was possible that a vehicle from the Home was stationed at the exit, waiting for us. But they had no description of our car, and for what seemed like an endless block, I kept the speed under control to cover up the fact that we were fleeing.

Then we pressed off again, into the night. Our crazy speed attracted the attention of a policeman, who followed us for a few blocks, but after we brutally ran an assailants' barricade on a dead-end street, the cop chose to concentrate on pursuing slower criminals. I couldn't find the air-conditioning button. I was sweating fiercely inside my seal suit. Underneath I still wore my own clothes like a second layer, now turned into an Eskimo torture device. We sweated in the suffocating air that blew in through the windows.

"Where are you going?" my father asked.

"I don't know. I'm getting out of the city."

"Well, I know. Give me the wheel."

"What for?"

"I've got a map. You'll go with me as far as the city limits, and then you'll come back."

"You believe in that crap, too?"

"Stop and give me the wheel, or I'll take it by force and we'll crash. It's all the same to me."

I couldn't convince him; he wouldn't listen. We struggled until I gave in. We were on a highway. I asked him to wait until we got to the first exit. His little nurse friend at the Home had told him about the community of Old Runaways and had given him a map and the password. He was right about one thing: why not try it? What awaited us in the city except more insane persecution? I patted my side to feel the reassuring weight of my gun, but it wasn't there. How strange. At the party, the presence of its pound-and-a-half bulk in my pocket had comforted me.

The seal suit decided it. I had reached the limits of what my body would endure. I would have paid in blood to take off the costume. I left the highway at the first exit, hit the brake, and began to peel off the disguise. My first impulse was to hand Papa the wheel, leaving him the stolen car, and to quietly remove myself from danger.

"You want to go. It's only logical. You're going to leave me alone," my father said as I stopped the car. As usual, he could read my thoughts with such bitter conviction that I couldn't help arguing with him.

"That's what you would do in my place."

My father regarded me with an enormous smile. I couldn't—didn't want to—decide if what he was trying to convey to me in that display of his beautiful false teeth was gratitude, irony, or affection.

28

We were on the Pan-American Highway heading toward Del Viso. My father hadn't touched a steering wheel in more than thirty years. He drove like a kid at an amusement park. My desperate attempts to get him off the road included a promise to take him anywhere he wanted to go. It was a sincere promise: having run over one of Goransky's dwarfs in a stolen car, I didn't have too many options.

There was no problem driving on the highway, but no one would have chosen to exit near Del Viso. It was an occupied zone. Once outside the capital, areas of no-man's-land were practically nonexistent. There were gated communities, occupied zones, villas, and nothing else. In the gated communities, the owners didn't like to hire local people. They brought in personnel from the city. Takeovers generally started from within, led by service workers, sometimes with the help of security guards if these weren't chosen carefully.

Once I spent a weekend in Highland, one of the nicest country clubs in the area, at the home of some friends. From that time on, I often dreamed we could be together, you and I, in a place like that: your naked body in the swimming pool, breaking the water in a perfect crawl, endowed with an athlete's powerful grace, gliding along effortlessly. Afterward, drops of water on your breasts, beading up at first and then slowly evaporating in the sun. When I told you my dream, you said you never did learn to swim with style, and you'd be embarrassed to swim naked: as though arguing about a dream made any sense. But you always found fault with my dreams; you dismissed them, you were afraid to let them stand, as if some part of them, a too-tall tower, could penetrate reality, as suspicious as the tip of an iceberg suddenly surfacing in the middle of a tropical rain forest.

When we arrived that day, we saw a large group of shabbily dressed women, some with their children, waiting outside the wire fence. It was close to noon, and the sun beat down fiercely on their sweaty faces. Several of them were huddled together like cattle in the shade of a billboard. They were waiting for some lady to choose them for day labor or for weekend work. There were also a few men offering their services for heavy labor or maintenance.

"One day," my friend remarked, "they'll all rise up, and that'll be it."

The very young women, the elderly ones, those with children, were at a disadvantage, but they also had fewer ambitions. Every summer some of those children would drown in the privately owned swimming pools because they didn't know how to swim like the members' kids, because many of the pools were unsupervised, and because their mothers were busy working and had neglected to watch them for a moment.

That night in Highland, I had trouble falling asleep, and after a while, I awoke to the sound of drums. It lasted for many hours. The dull, violent reverberation of the instruments mingled with the croaking of frogs and isolated cries and songs that I couldn't quite decipher. I mentioned it at breakfast. My friends laughed.

"They're the street musicians. The street music of Del Viso. They spend the entire year rehearsing for Carnival."

I took a look at the map my father showed me and realized this was our destination. We were going to Highland. Six hundred luxury homes with gardens and swimming pools, converted into an occupied zone, like the rest of Del Viso.

Shortly before we arrived, we passed Miraflores, which has been able to remain a gated community since it's located on the main road. Surrounded on all sides, it's easier to defend than Highland. In order to protect themselves, the Highland homeowners not only would have required guards on the outskirts but also would have had to establish and defend an access road for their armored vehicles, something almost impossible—or at least too expensive—to do in an occupied zone.

I was frightened when we left the highway. The intermittent thrum of the crickets was as terrifying as the silence. The moon was out. Despite the absence of street lighting, I could see farms and weeds at the sides of the road. I was really surprised when we were about to bump into my memories, so unchanged by the new reality of wire fences and a guard station.

But the protected, enclosed area was much smaller than what I remembered. At the guard station, we were greeted by a couple of old women armed with Uzis. When they heard the password, they lowered their weapons but didn't put them down. They made us get out of the car, and the one who was closer to us patted us down, fairly perfunctorily, with her stiff, clumsy hands, while the other one stood at attention.

"It's awfully hot, isn't it?" she remarked. "Has it always been so hot this time of year? Or is it just that we've forgotten?"

"No, it gets hotter every year. It's global warming," I replied. "It's because they're cutting down the Amazon rain forest."

That's the type of repartee that helps you get along with people.

In the darkness it was hard to tell them apart: like babies, old folks all look alike. In addition to searching for weapons, they ran their hands over my father's face, through his hair and beard, to make sure it wasn't makeup. By the light of the powerful flashlight they shined on us, I saw the red bloodstain that was already turning brown on the left bumper and fender. We told our story. One of the women climbed into the car with us and pointed the way to the leaders' residence.

There were no more than fifteen or twenty houses inside the wire enclosure. The soccer field had been planted over. The gardens had changed. The streets were dark. They didn't have too much electricity. Nevertheless, many houses were lit up.

"We old folks sleep differently," our guide explained. "As long as people here do their work, no one is obliged to sleep when they don't feel sleepy or stay awake when they need a nap. Fuck sleeping pills."

She was fat, dressed in a sort of shapeless bag, as comfortable and ridiculous as a nightgown. The house was very close by. The wire fence barely protected the entrance to Highland, where the soccer field and the properties were larger. The old residents called this section the *quintas*, or "country estates."

The house where they led us was well-maintained on the outside. The slate roof and brick, which had lasted for so many years, had preserved it from signs of neglect. A wide, pavilion-shaped porch, supported by a column, was the legacy of its original owners, who undoubtedly had tried to imitate the mansions in North American TV series.

Our elderly guide exchanged passwords with the occupants, and we went inside the house. The interior was in pathetic condition. The elegant "country" furnishings, made by the best carpentry firms in the city, who used to decorate clubhouses, had been replaced by authentic country furniture: crude, clumsy, poor, ugly, practical. A single, dusty, built-in sideboard remained, stained and marred by cigarette burns. Everything was damaged in one way or another. The light fixtures were broken or dented; a door hung loose on its hinges. I didn't even want to think about the condition of the bathrooms. The large living-dining room had been converted into a storage area for fruit and vegetables. Bags of potatoes were stacked in the cold fireplace; there were several barrels of apples, and a gigantic pile of onions reached almost to the ceiling. An ageless old man dozed, half-propped up, in the remains of an armchair. Every so often he produced a sound more like a death rattle than a snore.

The woman who let us in was comparatively young: she must have been slightly over seventy. I wondered what accident had landed her in a Convalescent Home. She looked healthy now: just a slight limp. She had been playing Solitaire at the large table. Lots of people that age still prefer board games: the manipulation of objects. She regarded us curiously, her eyes half shut. Papa, impatient as usual and fed up with the silence, interrupted the scrutiny.

"Are you in charge? Do the Old Runaways live here?"

"No one's in charge," the old woman said, but it was a lie. She spoke authoritatively and with class. "They call us the 'Old Runaways,' but it's a misnomer. There aren't too many old people here, and very few men. We women live longer."

"So much the better. I like women," my father said.

"That's bullshit. Nobody likes old women. But lots of people are afraid of us. They think we're witches. The local people don't mess with us. They respect us because they need us. We've got doctors, computer experts, a good electrician. We barter services. And you? What do you know how to do?"

"I know how to buy and sell things better than anyone else."

"If that's true, it'll come in handy. How do you plan to buy your way in?"

I hadn't worried about emptying the pockets of my costume before leaving it along the road. Now I didn't even have my credit cards on me. I regarded my father in desperation. We would have to resume our absurd flight.

"I brought morphine," my father said.

He pulled out the little packets of medication that I had gotten him when I rescued him from the Home. So he could die in peace.

For a moment, the woman's eyes sparkled with wild joy. Her hands crept toward the packets like animals moving of their own volition. Not all the packets were there. Papa had reserved two or three for the moment when he would need them, or perhaps in order to buy something else with them. The woman struggled to control herself, feigning indifference.

"Anything else?"

My father pointed to me.

"We need labor, young blood."

"Papa, I haven't been young in years," I laughed.

But the two of them looked at me scornfully. Everything is relative.

"I'm not his father," my father said. "I forced him to bring me here."

And he displayed my lovely Smith and Wesson Sigma, which he had managed to conceal during the stupid security check. Would he be capable of shooting me with it? This was the moment to find out. It was the moment to push them violently, to run away as they lay on the floor. Old people can't get up easily. But my astonishment or fear didn't allow me to react in time. Not quickly enough to avoid Papa's winking at me. An automatic response was triggered inside me, and I returned his wink with a half-smile, hiding it from the woman in complicity. I pretended to be scared and put up my hands. My father had invited me to be his accomplice, and I had fallen into the trap once more, proud and contented, like a good son.

Like an idiot.

29

For the first time, I have the feeling I'm really writing letters. I like it. It's one of the effects of writing longhand. There are others: a cramped hand and a painful wrist. For years I didn't write anything longhand except the occasional number, a name, a couple of words. It's a matter of exercise, like any physical labor, but field labor isn't the best exercise for relearning how to hold a pencil. Manual labor toughens my joints. For a while, my hands were blistered and sore; now they have calluses.

With an optimism that time rendered absurd, Bradbury, in *Fahrenheit 451*, anticipated a world in which it was necessary to forbid literature, so that readers would disappear. That same optimism caused him to imagine a marginalized community of readers with excellent recall, like living books, a sort of paradise for good, intelligent, sensitive, and generous people. The mad illusion that good readers are better than other human beings.

The Old Runaways aren't any better than other human beings. They're old: their virtues have diminished, and their defects have intensified. They share a strange indifference to the suffering of others that young people find hard to comprehend. Other people's deaths don't affect them. They're greedy, suspicious, they hate one another, and they're locked in a permanent, silent battle for power.

The Highland *quintas* have been converted into real country estates. The old folks occupy about twenty houses. The parks, gardens, and fields aren't large enough for extensive grain cultivation, but they have some magnificent orchards.

Don't think I've discovered any hidden pleasure in field work. I've always been a city rat. I hate the country—the dogs, the bugs, the animals. I even hate the trees, which is unusual. I hate pulling weeds, plowing the earth; I hate hoeing, digging, planting seeds. But I can't help admitting, I take pleasure and even pride in harvesting, despite the effort: real food, produced by my hands.

There aren't many of us workers. "Workers" is what the old folks call us. But we're slaves. They need us: it would be too dangerous to hire people from the occupied zone. I recognize the others from a distance; they don't allow us to get together. We sleep separately, locked in the tool sheds. We work the earth; we take care of the few animals; we do repair work in the houses. The old folks won't allow us to be used for their personal care, not even for the invalids. They prefer to cooperate among themselves, pushing each other around in wheelchairs, cleaning the bedsores of the bedridden, cooking for those who can't do it themselves, caring for the demented, the senile. They're sensibly cautious of the dangerous proximity that exists between servant and master.

My father still maintains our relationship secretly. In front of the others, he treats me harshly, but not so much as to attract attention. Here everyone pretends to love and to have been deeply loved by their children. The old women, especially, speak of them constantly, like another form of competition. Listening to them, I ask myself what kind of father I might have been, when I myself was a sort of eternal, tedious child who lived only to conquer his own father or to prove him wrong.

On the rare occasions when no one can see him, Papa drowns me in that sticky tenderness he's always used to get what he wanted.

"Ernie, my boy," he says. "I'm too old. The oil is drying up in my lantern. Can't you see how my light is going out? We'll have to hold out a little longer, just until they get tired of searching for me. Then we'll go away together; I'll talk to my lawyer; we'll leave the country."

I don't answer him. He wants to keep all his options open. Meanwhile, he doesn't have it too bad. He wears plaid shirts and blue overalls that he probably doesn't work in because they're always spotless. Someone is in charge of caring for him and serving him.

I want to kill him.

We all say things like that sometimes about someone we hate fiercely for a few moments, in a fit of childish rage. I want to kill him. Then the rage passes, the moment passes; life goes on, and we return to our normal selves: adult individuals—intelligent, tolerant, unwilling to take the trouble or risk of killing anyone.

Many times I've felt like killing my father. Killing him painlessly. Cutting his body into pieces, burning it, destroying it, making it disappear from this world.

When you decided to leave, for example, so that I wouldn't have to choose between him and you. But then you left, and I didn't do it.

When I thought he was dying, for example. I wanted to give him a very sweet death, kill him out of love: I never had such an excuse before. Maybe that's why I didn't do it.

Now I want to kill him without excuses. I want to kill him in order to restore the original order of the universe. I want to kill him to free myself of him and to force him to obey the law of life, which he resists. I want to kill him so I'll never have to hear him laugh again; I want to kill him because he enslaved me in every possible way; I want to kill him so I won't see him eat with that vital, repulsive greed with which he clings to this world; I want to kill him because you once desired him; I want to kill him because I feel like it.

I want to kill him.

30

I saw everything dimly, through smoke: the dirty floor of the hall,
the sooty walls, the fetid lamps. I was dizzy and blindfolded when
they took me from the cage and the judge picked me up to weigh
me. I was blindfolded, blindfolded: I saw everything dimly, through
smoke. The judge stuck his hand into my feathers, touched my spurs.
I knew Papa was right.

I applauded and applauded, twenty piasters for Zambo, I shouted,
twenty million piasters, piasters piasters and doubloons. Piasters. I
was Zambo, and I was betting on Zambo. Blood coursed through
my veins as though looking for an escape, my heart strong and swift,
my heart pumping a dense, black, viscous liquid. I moved my blood-
engorged arm up and down, and I knew that if I stopped moving it,
it would wither, turn into a dry, black strip. Then I moved it, moved
my arm, so that the blood would keep flowing to my fingers, looking
for an escape.

I felt my small, warm body when they placed it on the table; my
body twitched, twisted in my hands, I held it for a moment longer,
immobilizing it, but it needed air, I needed air, needed my air because
of the damn smoke from the lamps, the cigars. Then they removed
my blindfold. I saw him I saw him I saw him, there he was shaking
his wings and puffing up his neck feathers. We tottered; I thought the
struggle would be brief. I upped the ante; I had to win. I applauded
we applauded. With a terrible thrust of his spurs, he ripped off half
my comb and tore out one eye, but it was all right, it was all right
like that. I knew my father was right, I knew I deserved it, the pain
was very clear, it tasted like thick, sweet blood, I could see in spite
of everything. I even saw what was going on behind me. I saw the

bettors shouting, I heard their voices. Papa was among them and he was right, he was right. I was the one who was wrong.

I lifted Zambo, I lifted my own body into the air, my skinny legs dangling in midair, skinny, but with their terrible spurs. I raised the bottle and washed out my injured eye with whisky, I felt a burning, stinging pain; I trusted my sharp spurs; I flung myself against him. They were applauding me, I was bleeding, my feathers were dripping, dripping on the table, the opponent evaded me swiftly, throwing himself on top of me and striking me again with his spurs, smoke, shouts.

My hand was asleep, that tingling; I had to keep moving my arm rhythmically in order to pump the blood from my hand to my shoulder, from my shoulder to my hand. Once again he, my enemy, tried to dig his spur into my head, but I got away. I applauded they applauded, hurrahs, shouts, my father was right, my father hadn't bet on me, he hadn't bet on me. With a deft thrust of my beak, I pulled out one of his neck wattles, how horrible. A wattle—I pulled out one of his wattles, I rolled on the floor, shouting ecstatically, I made a bet, I rolled beneath the opponent's feet, his feet, and I saw his beak and I wanted his beak to dig into my throat, I wanted to rest, but I made a bet, a bet, there was a lot of money at stake, even more than life. A wattle, a wattle from his throat.

I broke away from his enormous weight on my chest, there's not enough air to breathe, to breathe, forgive me, I shouldn't have broken away but I was desperate to breathe, forgive me. A wattle, I yanked a wattle from his throat. I could stand wounds, yes, pain, yes, but you can't control asphyxiation, forgive me, it wasn't my fault, it's not me, it's just my body, I didn't want to break free, but my body freed itself, I escaped, so tiny, I climbed up his enormous bulk, slick with blood, he was nearly dead, amorphous material oozed from his throat, feces, gray vomit from his throat which was missing a wattle, a wattle. I grew, I grew with a thrust of my spurs, the last one, I bashed his head in—but why, when he was already dead? He was already escaping through his throat, flying away, but I bashed his head in anyway and crowed raucously, announcing my victory, while my father collected the bets. Then I didn't win, after all. I vomited whisky. I woke up I woke up I woke up. A wattle, a wattle.

I woke up, still not knowing what a wattle was, and my dream hadn't been just a dream.

I woke up with no air, no relief. I woke up, and it was today: the last day. They day when I'll give my father what he begged me for, weeping: rest, peace, solitude.

Or else I will receive it at his hands, and it will be the same thing.

I'll be in the orchard. I'll be working. I'll have the spade in my hand. The spade is very old. Its concentrated weight is almost as easy to manage as a hammer's. Faster and easier to control than a beak, the spade is, although not as lethal.

It will happen in the orchard, at noon, under the sun, at the witching hour, the hour of the nymphs. Nymphs don't grow old, they don't use makeup, they don't have plastic surgery, they don't need to control their emotions in order to prevent lines from disfiguring their faces, all identical, smooth, perfect, and marmoreal. Nymphs receive and don't give, nymphs don't submit. It will happen in the silence of the sun, at noon.

Or else, at noon, I won't kill my father or try to. What I'll do is confront all mankind, as all men do. Do we men choose our fathers, after all? No real man lets himself be adopted without struggling, without braying. Locking horns, conquering all other men, becoming the father.

Or else I'll be there with the spade, at noon. He'll come to the orchard, at the appointed hour, my father will come so that I can cease to be his son.

He's not strong anymore, not as strong as I am, I tell myself. I'll take care of him: but he's a strong old man, and he's my father.

Working the earth, my body has changed so much. My arms are thicker, my shoulders broader, muscles I can't recognize suddenly stir beneath my skin, unexpectedly. But I'm almost old myself; the farewell has already begun for me, too: and he's my father.

I'm not trembling. I see all things visible and invisible with uncanny

162

precision. I look at my hands, flex my fingers, sense the air surrounding objects and all their edges cutting the air like knives. And he is my father. I see, I hear, I sense odors. I tried to read, and I succeeded. The letters fuse into words, the words take on meaning, organizing themselves into meaningful phrases. I can eat, I can breathe. Today is the day I will cease to be a son, and the air tastes like fire.

He's my father. And who of us can be sure he'll be able to raise his hand, his sword, dispassionately, with cold violence, with restraint, against his father?

Especially against mine.

Not only is he strong, not only is he my father, but he has my gun and he's carrying it. Once again I ask myself if he'd be capable of using it against me. Only in a case of extreme necessity, I tell myself. That's how my father is.

Today at noon, under the sun, at the hour of the nymphs, my father will come. He himself arranged to meet me in the orchard. He wants to leave. To contact his lawyer, recover his money, leave the country. He needs me again. My father will come, and I will confront him. In the only possible way: without words, and to the death.

Did I tell you I wanted to kill my father? I lied.

At noon, under the sun, I want to create a new world. I want to create a world for you: a world where you'd no longer have to choose, my darling. Where you wouldn't have to run away to avoid choosing.

Now it's not just the feeling that I'm writing a letter.

Now, for the first time, from the last place on earth, I *am* writing you a letter.

I don't know what your life is like; I don't know what I'll find when I see you, but I know I'm going to look for you to find something you won't be able to deny me: so that all this writing will have meaning. So you will read me.

Did I tell you I wanted to kill my father? I lied. The only thing I'm trying to do is to stop sharing this universe with him.

That's why I'm going to create a new world. A world that will come too late for everyone, a world with room for only him or only me, a world where I will be intensely happy, even if I have to observe it from the outside, a world where his death or mine will matter little. Because it's not death I'm after, just that new kind of universe, and if I have to invoke death in order to obtain it, death will be merely a consequence, nothing more than an adverse, unwanted reaction, a simple side effect.

I plan to keep writing; I'm going to write you many letters, just letters, and from now on, my words will be proof that the world I imagine is possible, as well as proof that I'm still in it, orphaned and as light as air, and that my true life has finally begun.

IN THE LATIN AMERICAN WOMEN WRITERS SERIES

To order or obtain more
information on these or other
University of Nebraska Press titles,
visit *www.nebraskapress.unl.edu*.